PIPER DAVENPORT

Saving the PREACHER'S DAUGHTER

DOGS OF FIRE: SAVANNAH CHAPTER BOOK 1

2017 Piper Davenport
Copyright © 2016 by Piper Davenport
All rights reserved.
Published in the United States

Sale of this book without a front cover may be unauthorized. If this book is coverless, it may have been reported to the publisher as "unsold or destroyed" and neither the author nor the publisher may have received payment for it.

Saving the Preacher's Daughter is a work of fiction. Names, characters, places, and incidents are the products of the author's imagination and are used fictitiously. Any resemblance to actual events, locales, or persons, living or dead, is entirely coincidental.

Model
Brett Young

Cover Art
Jackson Jackson

ISBN-13: 978-1974103584
ISBN-10: 1974103587

ACKNOWLEDGEMENTS

Liz Kelly:
Thanks again. Your insight is always so spot on!

Felicia Lynn:
Thanks for being such an amazing cheerleader!

All it took was one page and I was immediately hooked on Piper Davenport's writing. Her books contain 100% Alpha and the perfect amount of angst to keep me reading until the wee hours of the morning. I absolutely love each and every one of her fabulous stories. ~ **Anna Brooks – Contemporary Romance Author**

Get ready to fall head over heels! I fell in love with every single page and spent the last few wishing the book would never end! ~ **Harper Sloan, NY Times & USA Today Bestselling Author**

Piper Davenport just reached deep into my heart and gave me every warm and fuzzy possible. ~ **Geri Glenn, Author of the Kings of Korruption MC Series**

This is one series I will most definitely be reading!! Great job Ms. Davenport!! I am in love!! ~ **Tabitha, Amazeballs Book Addicts**

For Nicole

*You are... well, just the best.
I love you! Thanks for all your support!*

ONE

Willow

I PUSHED OPEN the doors to my father's offices and smiled at the church's receptionist.

"Hi, Eleanor."

My father was the reverend of the First Baptist Church in Viewpoint, South Carolina, a church of about two hundred, older, conservative members. Even though it was small, there was a separate building that housed the pastoral offices behind the main church. My dad was the nicest man I knew. He was probably the nicest man anyone in town knew. Since my mother died ten years ago, it had been the two of us against the world. After her passing, I had to help keep Dad focused on his work, and he tried his best to fill the role of a mother to a teenage girl. It wasn't easy for either of us, but we grew incredibly close as we grieved and healed together.

"Oh, hi sweetie. How are you doing?" Eleanor pushed her Bible aside and leaned across the counter.

Eleanor Torres had worked at the church since before my father had taken over and she was very, very sweet. A little dim and out of touch, but always kind. Her husband Sam was a deacon and their daughter Taylor helped out with the little kids on occasion.

"I'm great, thank you," I said. "How's your mom?"

"She's doing much better. Thank you for asking."

"Of course." I held up a small stack of paper. "Daddy asked me to bring in the sermon he printed last night. Is he free?"

"Sure, sure, go on back."

I nodded and headed toward my dad's office.

As I approached, I heard two angry voices, low enough I couldn't understand what they were saying, but loud enough to know they were arguing.

I frowned. My father never argued with anyone. The only time he raised his voice was when he was preaching…and that was really only when it was on the topic of sin or the book of Revelation.

Now, however, he was the aggressor.

"I told you, Richard, I was done with this conversation and if you continue to—"

"Hi, Daddy," I said, interrupting the altercation. I faced Richard Waters and forced a smile. "Mr. Waters."

Richard was one of our deacons, but (and I'm ashamed to admit this), I didn't like him. In fact, he scared me. I didn't get a good feeling from the man, and even though he had a lovely wife and a perfectly polite son, he flat out gave me the creeps.

"Mornin' Willow," Richard said in his thick Kentucky accent, and his eyes raked my body making me feel like I should cover up. "You look…*beautiful.*"

I swallowed and took a deep breath in an effort not to

shudder. "Thank you."

"Well, I best be goin'," he said, and I stepped back so he could pass.

My dad leaned down and kissed my cheek, then closed the door. "Hi, honey."

"Hi, Daddy." I handed him the paperwork he'd asked me to grab from the house. "Why were you fighting with Mr. Waters?"

"It's nothing. Just a disagreement on a Bible verse."

"That sounded much more heated than a disagreement on a Bible verse," I countered.

"It's my job to be patient and guide our flock in the right direction. I promise you, it wasn't a heated argument." He smiled and squeezed my arms. "Now. Are you and Brad going out tonight?"

"Yep." I grinned and glanced at my engagement ring. Almost two carats of perfection in a platinum band. Brad Aljets was my newly announced fiancé and I was in love with the perfect man. He and I had grown up in the church together and his faith in God was as strong as my father's. He came from a lovely family (his father was the deputy mayor), and we'd been dating (chastely) for a year. He'd proposed the Sunday before last in front of the entire congregation, and I couldn't have been happier. I was twenty-two years old, entering my senior year of college to become a teacher, and couldn't wait to start my life with Brad. I was working on being the perfect political wife, and I thought I was doing a pretty good job so far.

"What time is he picking you up?" My dad asked.

"Seven."

"Well, why don't I take you to lunch and make sure you're home in time to be spoiled?"

"I would love to go to lunch with you, Daddy, but I'm meeting Jasmine and Parker to start the wedding planning."

Jazz and Parker were my two closest friends. Their

families attended our church, and we'd been inseparable since third grade.

"Well, that's far more important."

I giggled. "Nothing's more important than you. I can reschedule—"

"Don't you dare. It's not every day my little girl plans a wedding."

I kissed his cheek. "I love you."

"Love you too, sweetheart."

"I better get going."

He nodded. "Make sure you drive west…"

"So I avoid the biker bar," I repeated for the umpteenth time. The church was in a shady part of town…sort of. The biker bar was *literally* on the other side of the train tracks, which separated the "bad" part of town from our side of town. And the distance between the church and the bar was about four-hundred yards, but it was enough (to my father) to separate good from bad. West vs. east. Sometimes I wondered if Dad was worried there might be a "rumble." Maybe the Sharks and the Jets would break out in a knife fight…or even worse, in song and dance.

I bit back a giggle and sighed. "I know, Daddy. Don't worry. I'm careful."

"That's my girl." He sat behind his desk. "Text me when you get wherever you're going."

"I will. See you tonight."

He nodded and I decided to leave via the door from his office, rather than heading back through the lobby. It was faster and it meant I could avoid Richard Waters who usually hung around to speak with Eleanor whenever he visited.

As I walked to my car in the front, a deafening roar had me frozen in place.

A sea of black and chrome motorcycles flew by me, passing right in front of the church, and I couldn't help myself from laying my hand over my racing heart. My word, they were loud…and intimidating…and kind of exciting. I shoved that thought deep down in my soul. I was not allowed to think they were exciting. They were dangerous and the bikers certainly were not good people (as Brad had told me on more than one occasion).

The problem with me, however, was that I found myself enamored by motorcycles and the men who rode them. I'd always been drawn to them. I couldn't tell you why, but one of my earliest memories as a child was pulling away from my mother in a mall parking lot and running toward a motorcycle parked near our car. We'd been visiting her sister in San Diego, and we were getting a few supplies for our Disneyland visit the following day.

There was an older man with long hair and an even longer beard who saw me coming (probably because my mother let out a scream of fear), and knelt down to my level as I laid my hand on the bike.

"*Pretty.*"

He grinned. "*You like my hog, huh?*"

I nodded.

"*This here's a Harley Davidson Fatboy.*"

I wrinkled my nose. "*It's not nice to say 'fat.'*"

He chuckled. "*No, I don't suppose it is.*"

I stared at the man and knew I'd never forget his eyes. Ever. They were blue and they were kind…like Daddy's.

"*Willow!*" *my mother admonished.* "*Do not run away from me again.*"

"*Sorry, Mama. I like the hog.*"

"*The what?*" *she asked, and the man stood back up.*

"*My bike. I call it a hog.*"

"*Oh,*" *Mama said, and tugged me closer to her legs.* "*Well, thank you for letting her look at your motorcycle.*"

"*My pleasure, ma'am.*"

Mama pulled me (reluctantly) to our car and we drove away, never to see the man or the motorcycle again.

Brought back to the present by one of the bikers looking my way, I licked my lips and waited for the last bike to drive out of view. I noticed the patches on the backs of their jackets read: Dogs of Fire: Savannah, and it sounded kind of tame for a motorcycle gang. I suppose there was the fire bit, but no mention of Satan or pictures of nude women on their vests. I shook off my thoughts and climbed into my car, driving the opposite way of the men.

* * *

Dash

AS I PASSED the Baptist Church, I couldn't help but notice the leggy blonde standing by an older model Toyota Tercel. Fuck me, she was gorgeous.

She wore a thin, yellow sundress that stopped at her knees, and some sweater thing that covered her arms. She'd finished off the innocent as fuck lookin' outfit with cowboy boots and I suddenly felt pressure against my zipper. I imagined myself fucking her right out of the slip of fabric she called a dress, but I'd insist she keep those boots on.

word, they were loud...and intimidating...and kind of exciting. I shoved that thought deep down in my soul. I was not allowed to think they were exciting. They were dangerous and the bikers certainly were not good people (as Brad had told me on more than one occasion).

The problem with me, however, was that I found myself enamored by motorcycles and the men who rode them. I'd always been drawn to them. I couldn't tell you why, but one of my earliest memories as a child was pulling away from my mother in a mall parking lot and running toward a motorcycle parked near our car. We'd been visiting her sister in San Diego, and we were getting a few supplies for our Disneyland visit the following day.

There was an older man with long hair and an even longer beard who saw me coming (probably because my mother let out a scream of fear), and knelt down to my level as I laid my hand on the bike.

"Pretty."

He grinned. "You like my hog, huh?"

I nodded.

"This here's a Harley Davidson Fatboy."

I wrinkled my nose. "It's not nice to say 'fat.'"

He chuckled. "No, I don't suppose it is."

I stared at the man and knew I'd never forget his eyes. Ever. They were blue and they were kind...like Daddy's.

"Willow!" my mother admonished. "Do not run away from me again."

"Sorry, Mama. I like the hog."

"The what?" she asked, and the man stood back up.

"My bike. I call it a hog."

"Oh," Mama said, and tugged me closer to her legs. "Well, thank you for letting her look at your motorcycle."

"My pleasure, ma'am."

Mama pulled me (reluctantly) to our car and we drove away, never to see the man or the motorcycle again.

Brought back to the present by one of the bikers looking my way, I licked my lips and waited for the last bike to drive out of view. I noticed the patches on the backs of their jackets read: Dogs of Fire: Savannah, and it sounded kind of tame for a motorcycle gang. I suppose there was the fire bit, but no mention of Satan or pictures of nude women on their vests. I shook off my thoughts and climbed into my car, driving the opposite way of the men.

* * *

Dash

AS I PASSED the Baptist Church, I couldn't help but notice the leggy blonde standing by an older model Toyota Tercel. Fuck me, she was gorgeous.

She wore a thin, yellow sundress that stopped at her knees, and some sweater thing that covered her arms. She'd finished off the innocent as fuck lookin' outfit with cowboy boots and I suddenly felt pressure against my zipper. I imagined myself fucking her right out of the slip of fabric she called a dress, but I'd insist she keep those boots on.

TWO

Willow

BRAD ARRIVED AT seven on the dot. I was still wearing my yellow sundress, mostly because it was new and I loved it, but I'd changed out of my boots and wore a pair of strappy heels.

"Hi," I said, and Brad kissed me quickly before walking inside.

"Hi, sweetheart." He looked me up and down. "The dress is a little short, don't you think?"

I frowned. "Is it?"

"Yes."

"But I *love* this dress."

"Okay," he said with a quiet sigh. "If you like it." Then added, "And you think that's the best decision."

"I *do* like it, but if you want me to change, I will."

"Never mind, we don't have time," he said. "I'll just say hi to your father and we can go."

Well, now I felt like crap, but I trusted Brad and knew he didn't say it to hurt my feelings. He loved me. Brushing off my melancholy, I followed him into the den where Dad was on his computer and waited for them to say their hellos.

My dad chuckled. "Well, hi there, soon to be son-in-law."

"Alfred." Brad shook his hand. "Good to see you."

"Where are you heading tonight?"

"Chez Orange."

"Oh-ho, fancy."

Brad wrapped an arm around my waist and smiled. "Our girl deserves it."

I blushed, my heart warming. "Thanks, honey."

He gave me a gentle squeeze and I let out a quiet, "Sorry, darling." Brad *hated* "honey." He'd asked me to call him love or darling, but honey was off the table. I kept forgetting, but was glad he was patient with me.

"Well, we better get going," Brad said. "Our reservation is in twenty minutes."

My dad kissed me on the cheek. "Have a great time."

"Thanks, Daddy," I said, and followed Brad out of the house.

He held the door for me and I slid into the car, careful of my "short" dress. He walked to his side and climbed in, securing his seatbelt.

"How was your day?" I asked as we drove.

"Good. How was yours?"

I sighed. "Fun. Jazz, Parker, and I went looking at dresses."

He smiled. "Did you find anything?"

"Not yet." I waved my finger in the air. "But I will."

He chuckled. "Are you excited?"

I smiled. "Very excited. Are you?"

"Yes. I love you, Willow."

"I love you, too."

We arrived at the popular and expensive French restaurant in downtown Savannah, and I waited for Brad to collect me. As we walked inside, he took my arm in his (he felt holding hands was too 'high school' and public displays of affection were gauche), and then guided me in front of him so he could hold the door.

Brad spoke with the Maître D' and then he guided me in front of him again to follow the man to our table.

After Brad ordered for me, I tried to broach the subject of our living situation once we were married. I really wanted to stay close to my father, however, he had his eye set on a mansion by the water. The thought made me cringe, to be honest. I understood my place as the wife of a politician (he was currently vying for a seat in the senate), and we'd need to entertain some very important people, but I liked people.

People of all kinds, not just the rich or the pretty.

The thought of being alone in a gigantic house while the rest of my friends were an hour away and working, was tough to swallow. I'd be isolated and I knew myself well enough to know that, as an extrovert, it would kill me.

Before I could say anything, however, a man and a woman walked toward us and my breath left my body. I knew him. At least, I thought I knew him…How did I know him?

He had long hair and a long beard, tattoos and a rough look about him. Despite his clean, dark jeans and button-up shirt, I had a feeling this wasn't his usual attire. They were seated at the table next to us, in a u-shaped booth, and I watched as he slid to the middle, wrapping an arm around the woman to pull her close and kiss her temple.

The woman was a beautiful and graceful blonde. She

wore a dress similar to mine, only a little shorter and a lot more low-cut. She was stunning and wholly enamored with her date. I took a slow, deep breath. I wanted that.

"They will let anyone in nowadays," Brad hissed under his breath.

"*Brad*," I whispered.

He frowned. "What?"

"Please don't be rude."

He sighed and leaned forward. "If you can't afford to eat here every day, and dress appropriately for the event, then you shouldn't bother."

"How do you know he can't afford to eat here every day?" I challenged.

"Look at him. He looks like one of those bikers."

Well, he had me on that. He *did* look like one of 'those bikers.' He was sexy. I bit my lip. I shouldn't notice those kinds of things.

"Bikers can't afford to eat at expensive restaurants?" I asked.

Brad shot me a look without comment.

"And does he need to sit so close?" Brad continued. "I didn't come here to watch an erotic film."

I blushed. I'd never seen an erotic film, but that didn't mean I wasn't tracking with him. "They're obviously in love. I think it's sweet."

"Lust is more like it," he ground out. "It's disgusting."

"Would you like to leave?" I asked.

"No," he said with a sigh. "I won't let the likes of him ruin my evening."

I stared at him. I couldn't believe that a couple enjoying a romantic dinner would register on the things that would 'ruin' Brad's evening. It bothered me. Enough that I sat quietly and picked at my salad. I couldn't stop covertly glancing at the other table. They were so in love. She giggled a lot while he whispered to her, close to her ear, kissing her cheek, her neck, her lips.

My heart raced and my nether regions tingled. Good Lord, he was sexy.

"Willow," Brad rasped.

"Sorry, what?" I asked.

He sighed. "You're angry with me."

"No, not at all."

"Why are you so quiet, then? I usually have to ask you to stop talking."

I forced myself not to scowl at him. "Would you excuse me for a minute? I have to use the ladies' room."

I rose to my feet (as did Brad) and I headed to the bathroom. I was suddenly so angry I could spit. Not the appropriate emotion for a future senator's wife.

As I was washing my hands, the lady with the sexy man walked in. She gave me a lovely smile and said, "I absolutely love your dress."

She was British. Of course she was. She simply oozed class.

"Thank you so much," I said. "I was thinking the same thing of yours."

"My husband surprised me with it today...along with a weekend away without the children."

"That's so sweet," I said. "You look very happy together."

She nodded, her expression growing dreamy. "He's the best man I've ever known."

"Have you ever been to Savannah before?"

"No. It's beautiful. I feel like three days won't be enough time."

We chatted for a few more minutes and I gave her a few "locals" favorites, then headed back to the table, nearly running into her husband.

"Sorry, babe. Didn't mean to startle you," he said.

"You didn't." I smiled.

"My wife still in there?"

I nodded. "Yes."

"You okay?"

"Yes. Ah..." I frowned. "Sorry, I'm being rude."

"How exactly are you being rude?"

"I've been taught staring is rude."

"I'm flattered you're starin' at me," he joked.

"It's just that you look very familiar to me."

He crossed his arms. "Oh, yeah?"

"I can't quite place it."

"Well, since I've never been to Savannah, I'd imagine it's not me who's familiar."

I sighed. "Maybe not."

"Hatch, stop flirting."

I turned to see the blonde walking toward us. Hatch chuckled. "Was makin' sure you didn't fall in."

"Oh, you're hilarious," she retorted.

I blushed...again. "Well, I should get back to my fiancé."

"He's a handsome young man," the blonde said.

"Thank you."

"I'm Maisie, by the way," she said, reaching her hand out.

I shook it and smiled. "Willow."

"Oh, that's such a gorgeous name," she breathed out.

"Thank you. Mama loved it as well," I said, my heart a little sad. "I really hope you enjoy Savannah. I certainly love living here."

"Thank you for the suggestions," she said.

"You're welcome." I left them in the hallway and made my way back to the table. Brad stood as I approached and held my chair for me, leaning down to kiss my cheek quickly before taking his own.

I was a little surprised...he never showed me any kind of affection in public. I liked it. I liked it very much.

Hatch and Maisie returned to their table a few minutes after me and Maisie shot me a sweet smile. I focused back on Brad and we finished our dinner.

Once Brad paid the check, we rose to leave just as Hatch called out, "Nice to meet you, Willow."

I smiled, but Brad looked like he was about to combust. "Let's go," he snapped.

I glanced at Hatch, I don't know why, but when I did, I saw his expression form a scary glare toward my fiancé. He moved to leave the table, but Maisie grabbed his arm.

I gasped, ignoring Brad's order. "Give me a second," I said, and walked to their table.

"You okay, babe?" Hatch asked.

"Huh?"

"Your...companion. Not likin' the way he's talkin' to you."

"Oh, he's fine. He blusters sometimes." I waved my hand dismissively. "Were you ever in San Diego?"

"Used to live there."

"Do you have a Harley...um...Fatboy?"

"Yeah, why?"

"Because I think I've met you...in a mall parking...I'm not sure where. I was little, but I remember a motorcycle and running toward it, and then the next day we went to Disneyland."

"Were you with your mom? And you told me it was mean to say 'fat.'"

"Yes," I said excitedly. "It *was* you! I knew I'd never forget your eyes."

He grinned. "Oh, yeah?"

"You do have lovely eyes, darling," Maisie said.

"Willow," Brad growled, taking my arm. "We're leaving. *Now*."

"You need to get your hands off her," Hatch warned.

Brad released me immediately.

I could feel unadulterated rage pouring off my fiancé, so I slid my purse over my shoulder and smiled at Hatch and Maisie. "Well, it was very nice to meet you both. I hope you enjoy your visit."

"Thanks, love," Maisie said.

Hatch nodded, but continued to watch Brad closely as he turned and started toward the doors. I followed, a little apprehensive about his irritation, but not regretting having met the couple.

* * *

Dash

SATURDAY AFTERNOON, I was sittin' on one of the club's sofas, knockin' back my second beer, new girl on my lap (I think her name was Annette), and she'd just given me the blow job of a lifetime...hence the reason she was currently on my lap. If she was gonna work that hard to suck my dick, she deserved a little more quality time with me.

"Dash!" Badger bellowed.

I didn't move. "What?"

My fellow club brother stalked toward me. "Hatch and his woman are walkin' in."

"Shit." I set Annette aside and rose to my feet. "He's early."

"Yeah, man, I fuckin' know."

"Where's Doc?"

"He's runnin' late. He asked us to 'entertain.'"

"Fuck," I breathed out. "Hatch's woman's high-class."

Badger laughed. "Yeah, but she married Hatch, so she's gotta be cool...right?"

I glanced around the clubhouse. Pool table, bar, TVs with some football game on, and half-dressed women makin' out with half-baked and/or drunk club brothers. "Let's hope so," I grumbled, and we headed toward the front doors.

Hatch Wallace was the Sgt. at Arms for the Dogs of Fire in Portland...the original chapter. He'd been in the San Diego chapter before moving to Portland, and he was now visiting Savannah. He'd been close buddies with Doc, our president, so the official word was he'd decided to come out and assist with some club business, and bring Maisie for a few days to see the sights. That's all we knew, but I had a feeling something else was goin' on.

Hatch walked in ahead of his woman, but had her hand in his as they stepped into the lobby area of the clubhouse. Fuck me, his woman was smokin'. She was about five-feet-seven, blonde, legs for days, and she wore clothes that looked like they cost more than my bike. Shit, her sunglasses alone probably cost more than everything I own.

Introductions were made and Hatch pulled a jump drive from his pocket. "Doc's runnin' late," he said. "I told him I'd drop this by so he could look at it before we hook up with everyone at Barney's."

Barney's was our favorite hole-in-the-wall bar and pool hall. When we wanted to meet up with friends who weren't club brothers, or were members of other clubs, we went there. Barney's was known by all as neutral ground for all clubs, and tonight a bunch of us were meetin' to play pool and shoot the shit.

"He's gonna be here in twenty," I said. "You wanna wait?"

Hatch shook his head. "Promised Maisie we'd do some sightseeing shit."

"Oh, nice, love," she deadpanned, speaking like the fuckin' Queen of England. "Blame me."

He laughed. "Do I look like a man interested in touring every haunted mansion in Savannah?"

"If you know what's good for you, you will."

I forced myself not to grin. This bitch was hot *and* funny. Wicked combination.

"He can call me if he has any questions, but tell 'im I'll probably ignore him."

Badger chuckled. "Okay, man."

"It was lovely to meet you both," Maisie said.

"You too, babe," I said.

"We'll see you tonight," Hatch said, and headed back out the way he came.

I walked back into the common room to find my chick had moved on to another brother, so I grabbed a fresh beer and joined Badger at the pool table.

* * *

Willow

SATURDAY MORNING, I awoke with a heavy heart. Brad and I had had a pretty intense discussion last night and he'd left me on my doorstep without a kiss.

He was angry with me that I'd spoken with Hatch. It was not appropriate for a senator's wife to 'associate with those kinds of people.' When I pointed out I wasn't his wife yet, his face got a strange strangled look on it, and he'd turned and walked to his car. He didn't stay and hash it out. He didn't let me give him my point of view. He just left.

I remember stomping my foot in frustration before letting myself into the house. The thing about Brad was he was always well-behaved. He never raised his voice, he wouldn't do more than chastely kiss me, he *never* displayed public affection. His emotions were always controlled. Basically...he never showed passion of any kind and it was beginning to wear thin. Really thin.

"Button?" Dad called from his office as I walked downstairs for breakfast.

I peeked inside. "Hi, Dad. You're up early."

"I have to head to church in a bit."

"Is everything okay?"

"Of course. I just have to get some papers to Eleanor to copy for tomorrow's sermon." He smiled. "Did you have fun last night?"

I sighed. "Honestly? Not really."

I filled him in on the entire evening and he smiled.

"You'll work it out."

I nodded. "I know. I just wish he'd show some Christian kindness, you know?"

"He's just trying to protect you, honey. Cut him some slack."

"I will," I said, although, I wasn't sure I was telling the truth. "Want some coffee?"

"I've already had two cups." He pushed away from his desk. "I should head out."

"I'll swing by in a few hours and see if there's anything I can help with."

He cupped my face. "You're a good girl, Willow."

"My daddy raised me right."

"Oh, did he? Remind me to thank him should I ever meet the man," he said smiling playfully. He kissed my cheek and left the room.

I heard the lock on the door clank and then his car leave the garage. For the next three hours, I puttered around the house, checking my phone at least twenty times. No texts from Brad, and no responses to the three I'd sent.

Deciding I was done feeling sorry for myself, I grabbed my purse and took off to the church. There was always something happening on the weekends, so I was sure I could find something there with which to occupy my time.

About two miles from my destination, I felt a jolt and then my car rocked sideways and I knew I'd blown a tire. "Great!" I hissed. This was all I needed.

I really didn't want to get dirty changing a tire, but it was either that or walk to the church, and it was surface of the sun hot today, so I didn't have much of a choice.

I limped my car to the side of the road and popped the trunk, sliding out and walking to the back. After grabbing the jack and tire iron, I hefted the donut onto the pavement and slid my keys into my jeans pocket. Before I had a chance to hunker down, a roar had me looking toward the church...a motorcycle and its occupant was heading my way, probably coming from the bar.

I tented my hand over my eyes and watched as he pulled his bike up next to me. My heart raced as he climbed off and removed his helmet. Good lord, the man was beautiful. I shivered, suddenly feeling very guilty that I'd just thought that.

"You need some help?" he asked.

"No thank you."

He smiled and I found myself swallowing convulsively. "How about I change that tire for you and get you on your way before you melt?"

"I'm quite capable of changing my own tire."

"Don't doubt it, babe, but I happen to hold the record of quickest tire changer, and that's on a semi, so figure I could do it for you."

I bit my lip, trying not to smile. "Did you get a major award?"

"Fifty bucks, but no trophy or leg lamp. Felt a little gipped, to be honest. That lamp woulda looked great at the compound."

"Fifty dollars is a nice chunk of change."

He chuckled. "Bought a lot of beer."

"I'm sure you did."

He slid his leather jacket off and set it on the hood of my car. "Can't in good conscience leave you out here to fend for yourself."

He brushed past me, and before I knew it, my old tire was in my trunk, as were the jack and tire iron, and he was brushing off his hands as he approached me again.

"Wow," I said. "You weren't kidding."

He chuckled. "My name's Dash."

"Willow," I said. "Thank you for doing that. Can I pay you?"

"Hell, no. Just drive slow on that donut 'til you can get

a replacement tire."

"I will."

"You have far to go?"

I shook my head. "Just heading to the church."

"Right. Well, you drive slow, Willow."

"Thanks. I will."

I climbed back in my car and headed to church…my mind on a man who more than likely would never step foot in one. I walked into the building and peeked into my dad's office.

"Hey, sweetheart, everything okay?"

I nodded. "I was moping, so I thought I could come and help with the kids."

"There's my girl." He looked at his watch. "Bible study's going to start in about five minutes, I'm sure they could use you. A few extras showed up."

I nodded, deciding against telling my dad about the flat tire. If Dad knew I'd let a biker help me change it, I'd probably get an earful, so I figured I'd run down to Wal Mart on the way home and have them deal with it.

"I'll see you later."

"Okay, honey," he said, and I headed to the nursery.

THREE

Dash

A WEEK AFTER the incident with the sexy as fuck Willow, I backed my bike into a space in front of the bar and set my helmet over the handlebars before heading inside. Badger was hangin' with Shutter and Fletch in the back, so I walked toward them, stopping at the bar for a beer on the way.

Badger gave me a chin lift. "Hey, man."

"Hey. You get that shit sorted with the delivery?"

"Yeah. Doc's happy."

I nodded. "Cool."

The Dogs ran a few bars and nightclubs in the area and we'd been dealing with some issues with liquor delivery… there were a couple assholes who considered themselves part of the Dixie Mafia. They weren't mafia, so much as pains in the asses. The Mafia didn't claim them, but they certainly wanted to be part of it, so they continued to create trouble for the Club and other business owners in the area.

We racked a game of pool just as Hatch walked in with Doc and Doc's current obsession, Olivia Worthington. She was hot, and she seemed okay I guess, but she came from money, and none of us could figure out why Doc was chasing after her so hard. He'd always said he hated southern belles and their penchants for snobbery, and it wasn't like he needed her money.

Hatch was stayin' for another week to help deal with the delivery shit, but his woman had gone back to Portland to take care of the kids.

Everyone said their hellos and Doc headed to the bar to grab a drink for Olivia…that was when all hell broke loose.

The front door of the bar slammed open and a woman screamed, "Help me!" over the din of the music and voices. I stalked toward her and realized it was Willow. She was covered in blood, and clearly in shock, so I grabbed her gently and pulled her further into the bar.

"Ow," she squeaked, and I realized the blood was hers.

"What happened?" I demanded.

"Someone shot my dad," she rasped.

"Fuck me!" Hatch snapped. "Willow?"

"You know her?" I asked.

"We met a while ago," he said. "Doc, you got your shit?"

Doc was already moving to the door.

Willow fisted her hand in my shirt. "Help."

I laid my hand over hers and nodded. "I'm gonna help you."

"No. Daddy. Someone shot him."

"Badger!" I yelled over my shoulder. "Get a crew to

the church, make sure you're armed."

"On it," he said, and gathered the Dogs and a few guys from the Predators' crew, while I guided Willow to a chair.

She tried to move around me, but I held firm. "Wait, Willow, I need to check you—"

"No!" She pushed at my hands.

"Is there somewhere private we can go?" Olivia asked.

"Right," I said.

Willow craned her head toward the front door. "I need to check on—"

"No," I ground out. "We need to figure out where you're bleeding from."

She pushed at me again. "There were two."

"We're gonna figure it out, honey," Olivia promised.

Willow's face drained of color, and considering I was fairly familiar with the look, I caught her as she passed out. "Shit!" I hissed.

"Back here, Dash," Raven, one of the bartenders, said. "Bring her into the office."

I cradled her to me and carried her as gently as I could into the office, settling her on the sofa. Doc walked in a couple of minutes later and shoved me out of the way. He was an army medic and a licensed doctor, and since I knew I couldn't do anything to help her, I decided to head over to the church and see if I could figure out what happened. "Badger, let's go!"

The church was only minutes away, and I didn't hear sirens yet. Someone must've heard the shots, or seen something and called 911 by now. We parked our bikes and drew our guns before entering. I could smell gun powder and blood and it didn't take long to see why. A woman lay slaughtered in a pool of her own blood, behind her desk. She had at least two visible gunshot wounds to her head and chest. A young girl wasn't far from her… facedown, blood pooling around her head.

"Check the lady's pulse Badger."

He looked at me terrified. "She's fuckin' dead man! Are you fucking kidding me?"

"Just do it. I'm gonna check that room."

I knelt down and checked the young girl's pulse, couldn't find one, so I rose to my feet and headed down the hall. I entered a small office only to find another body, this time an older man, and even more blood. Blood on the walls, and on the floor. Whoever did this meant business. This was a straight up execution, but who the fuck would want to butcher a couple of old church people? I leaned down to check on the man.

"My daughter," his low voice wheezed causing me to jump.

I couldn't believe he was alive. "Badger! Call 911!" I bellowed and knelt beside him.

"Willow. My daughter," he rasped again, now pointing toward the open closet. I could see blood on the inside walls and figured that's where she was when the bullets started flying.

"She's okay, she's with us. We've got her and help is on the way. You just hold on, okay?"

"Willow."

"She's okay sir, she's okay."

"Please protect her," he whispered. "They'll come for her…"

"Who will? Who are they?" I pressed.

"Protect her. Protect Willow."

"We'll take care of her. I'll make sure she's okay. I promise. You just hang in there."

The last word the old man ever spoke was his daughter's name, in a sweet, concerned whisper. The next thing I heard was very different.

"Get the fuck down on the ground right now or I'll blow your goddamned head off!"

I heard the cop's voice before I'd even noticed the sirens.

"Get the fuck off me, man, we didn't do anything." I could hear Badger's protests from the other room. "Hey man, we called you! I was the one that called 911."

Badger's words fell on deaf ears. We were cuffed and stuffed, and I figured I'd better start getting used to the idea of breakfast at county tomorrow morning.

* * *

Willow

I COULDN'T BREATHE. I swam through the darkness trying to get away from the pain in my arm, but there was never any relief. I cried out as a sharp pain hit my flesh.

"Willow, it's Hatch. Wake up, babe."

"Hatch?"

"Yeah. Can you open your eyes?"

"Daddy," I rasped.

"Dash and Badger went to find out what's going on. Doc's going to give you something for the pain."

I swallowed. I was so thirsty, but before I could ask for water, I felt a prick on my arm and then relief. I sagged against whatever I was lying on.

"Shouldn't we call an ambulance?" a female voice asked. I wasn't sure who she was asking since my eyes were closed.

"No cops," a gruff voice said. "Her wound was through-and-through, I'll stitch her up and she'll be good to go. But until we know what the fuck happened, I'm not subjecting her, or us, to the local jerk-offs parading as law enforcement."

"Doc!" another deep voice bellowed.

"What?"

"Badger and Dash just got picked up."

I forced my eyes open and looked up at the man leaning over me. He turned toward the door and snapped,

"Check the lady's pulse Badger."

He looked at me terrified. "She's fuckin' dead man! Are you fucking kidding me?"

"Just do it. I'm gonna check that room."

I knelt down and checked the young girl's pulse, couldn't find one, so I rose to my feet and headed down the hall. I entered a small office only to find another body, this time an older man, and even more blood. Blood on the walls, and on the floor. Whoever did this meant business. This was a straight up execution, but who the fuck would want to butcher a couple of old church people? I leaned down to check on the man.

"My daughter," his low voice wheezed causing me to jump.

I couldn't believe he was alive. "Badger! Call 911!" I bellowed and knelt beside him.

"Willow. My daughter," he rasped again, now pointing toward the open closet. I could see blood on the inside walls and figured that's where she was when the bullets started flying.

"She's okay, she's with us. We've got her and help is on the way. You just hold on, okay?"

"Willow."

"She's okay sir, she's okay."

"Please protect her," he whispered. "They'll come for her…"

"Who will? Who are they?" I pressed.

"Protect her. Protect Willow."

"We'll take care of her. I'll make sure she's okay. I promise. You just hang in there."

The last word the old man ever spoke was his daughter's name, in a sweet, concerned whisper. The next thing I heard was very different.

"Get the fuck down on the ground right now or I'll blow your goddamned head off!"

I heard the cop's voice before I'd even noticed the sirens.

"Get the fuck off me, man, we didn't do anything." I could hear Badger's protests from the other room. "Hey man, we called you! I was the one that called 911."

Badger's words fell on deaf ears. We were cuffed and stuffed, and I figured I'd better start getting used to the idea of breakfast at county tomorrow morning.

* * *

Willow

I COULDN'T BREATHE. I swam through the darkness trying to get away from the pain in my arm, but there was never any relief. I cried out as a sharp pain hit my flesh.

"Willow, it's Hatch. Wake up, babe."

"Hatch?"

"Yeah. Can you open your eyes?"

"Daddy," I rasped.

"Dash and Badger went to find out what's going on. Doc's going to give you something for the pain."

I swallowed. I was so thirsty, but before I could ask for water, I felt a prick on my arm and then relief. I sagged against whatever I was lying on.

"Shouldn't we call an ambulance?" a female voice asked. I wasn't sure who she was asking since my eyes were closed.

"No cops," a gruff voice said. "Her wound was through-and-through, I'll stitch her up and she'll be good to go. But until we know what the fuck happened, I'm not subjecting her, or us, to the local jerk-offs parading as law enforcement."

"Doc!" another deep voice bellowed.

"What?"

"Badger and Dash just got picked up."

I forced my eyes open and looked up at the man leaning over me. He turned toward the door and snapped,

"Fuck!"

I jumped slightly and a pretty brunette squeezed my hand. "It's okay, Willow. My name's Olivia. We're going to take care of you. Doc just needs to finish stitching you up."

"Yeah," he said, smiling gently. "You're doin' great. Just close your eyes and relax."

I closed my eyes, not because he told me to, but because I couldn't keep them open.

"Doc!"

"Fuck me," he growled out. "What?"

"Cops are here."

"Stall 'em."

I felt tugging on my now numb arm, and then heard the snip of scissors, and I opened my eyes again. "Can you bandage her, Liv?"

"Yes, of course," she said.

"I'm gonna take care of this." Doc tugged off his gloves, rose to his feet, and left the room as Olivia grabbed gauze and bandages to wrap my arm.

"How does he know how to do that?" I asked.

"He's a doctor." She patted my arm. "A very good one actually."

"Oh," I whispered. I swallowed. My mind was jumbled and I was so thirsty, I also felt funny.

"Let's get you some water," Olivia said. "Morphine can make you thirsty."

"Then can we check on my dad?" I begged.

Olivia opened a bottle of water and handed it to me. "Let me find out, okay? Right now you're safe, and we want to make sure you stay that way."

"It was so loud."

"I bet that was really frightening," Olivia crooned.

I nodded. "My dad forced me into his closet to hide. I'm not sure how I got shot."

Hatch walked into the room and hunkered down in

front of me. I was both surprised and incredibly relieved to see him. "The cops are looking for you. They arrested two men and they need you to ID them."

"The men from the church? They were still there?"

"No. They arrested a couple of our guys."

I frowned. "Why?"

"They went to go check on your father, and the moron cops think they're the shooters."

"Where's my dad?"

"He's on his way to the hospital."

"So, he's not dead," I said, my heart beginning to calm a bit.

"They didn't say either way," Hatch said.

"Where are the police officers?"

"They left. We convinced them you weren't here to buy you some time. I can take you to the hospital if you want and you can figure out when to go down to the station."

"The police station is on the way to the hospital," I informed them. "Your friends shouldn't be in jail. I'll sort that out first. But can I please borrow a phone?"

"You can use mine." Olivia pulled hers out of her purse. "Here."

I found the number for the hospital and dialed it. After three transfers, I finally got through to someone in the emergency department. "I'm looking for my father."

"What's his name and the nature of the emergency?"

I gave her all the information I could about my father, but she seemed confused. "Ma'am, I'm sorry. No one with that name or description has been brought here. I can take your name and number and call you if he arrives."

"Okay. Um. This number is fine. My name is Willow. I'm his daughter."

"I'll call you as soon as I hear anything."

"Thank you." I hung up and handed the phone to Olivia. "They're going to call if they find him."

"I'll keep the phone close," she promised.

"Thank you." I rose tentatively, but Hatch caught me when I wobbled.

"Careful," he warned. "You've got some serious shit flowing through your veins."

I nodded and grasped his arm. I was suddenly freezing. "I need to find out what's going on."

"Can we find her a jacket?" Olivia asked no one in particular. "She's still in shock."

A young man settled a large, leather jacket over my shoulders and I slipped my arms into the warmth and pulled it close. I felt safe and secure in a weird way.

"Is there anyone we can ring for you?" Olivia asked.

"My phone is at the church," I said, shaking my head. "It's in my dad's office, and I don't have anyone's number memorized."

"Liv, you stay here," Hatch said to Olivia.

"Why?"

"Doc'll fuckin' kill me if you get dragged into this shit."

"I've kind of already been 'dragged into this shit,'" she countered.

"Um…sorry, but is it okay if she comes?" I asked. "I don't ride in cars alone with men I don't know."

"It's absolutely fine," Olivia said, somewhat forcefully.

Hatch sighed. "You'll stay close."

"Of course I will," Olivia promised.

Hatch wrapped his arm tightly around my waist and half carried me to their car, settling me inside gently and securing my seatbelt for me.

"You're gonna need to direct me, Willow. I don't know my way around."

"It's seriously right around the corner," Olivia answered for me. "Just turn left here and then right at the stop light. The police department will be on your left."

"Fuckin' small towns," Hatch retorted.

"You have no idea," Olivia said.

We pulled into the parking lot and Hatch set the brake.

"How about I take Willow inside?" Olivia said. "If they see you and know you lied, they might make things difficult."

He frowned. "Liv—"

"I will come and get you if there's a problem," she interrupted, jumping out of the car and opening my door. "Come on, honey. We'll get this sorted, eh?"

I nodded and followed Olivia into the station.

"Willow?"

I turned to find Lisa Walker, one of our parishioners walking toward me. As well as being a faithful church attendee, she was also one of the good and honest cops in town.

"Hi, Lisa," I said, relieved to see a friendly face.

"I'm so sorry about your dad."

"He's on the way to the hospital."

"No, he's not."

I frowned. "He's not?"

"Sweetie, I'm so sorry but your father didn't make it. He passed away."

I felt my knees buckle and Olivia caught me as I burst into tears. "That's why I couldn't find him at the hospital."

"We've been trying to reach you. He was sent to the coroner, and we need you to identify the body. I really am so sorry."

Lisa and Olivia helped me to one of the sofas in the lobby and I broke down. Olivia handed me a tissue and slid her arm across my shoulders.

"I can drive you over there if you'd like," Lisa offered.

I nodded, but then shook my head, my mind clearing a little bit. "I think you've arrested the wrong people. I ran to the biker bar next to the church and asked for help. Some of the men went to assist."

"Are you able to identify those men? We need to positively rule them out."

"I think so."

Lisa sighed. "You need to be sure, Willow."

The only one I knew I could identify for sure was Dash...and that was because I'd been dealing with some seriously inappropriate dreams about the man ever since he changed my tire.

"I'm sure."

"Okay. Let me figure out a line-up and then we can go see your father."

I nodded. "Thanks, Lisa."

Lisa left us in the lobby and walked through the secure door.

"Are you sure you want to do this right now?" Olivia asked.

"I need to."

"But perhaps your father is more important."

I shook my head, tears streaming down my face. "It won't change the fact that he's..." I couldn't say the words, so instead, I said, "Olivia, I don't want your friends in jail when they shouldn't be."

She squeezed my hand as I continued to sob in the lobby of the police station. I had never been so confused in my life. My mind was foggy and I knew part of it was from the meds, but mostly because I felt like I was in a nightmare I couldn't wake up from.

"Willow," Lisa called a few minutes later. "We're ready for you."

Olivia handed me another tissue and walked with me, her arm around my waist. I forced myself to control my tears and followed Lisa down a hall and into a dark room with a large window in it.

She pressed a button and said, "Send them in."

Six men walked in and stood facing the window. I recognized the man on the bike immediately. "Number three is the one who helped me...um, Dash. He definitely wasn't the shooter."

"You're sure."

"Yes, positive." I leaned forward. "And number five was behind the bar."

"You're sure?"

"Yes," I hissed in frustration. "They were there when I walked into the bar. Since I was still hearing gunshots when I ran, there's no way they could have been the shooters."

"What about the others?" Olivia asked.

"I'll ask the questions, ma'am," Lisa said.

"Sorry," she whispered.

"Do you recognize the others, Willow?" Lisa asked.

I shook my head. "No. The men who shot my dad were wearing all black. But these men are wearing jeans and vests with white T-shirts. I'm fairly certain they aren't shooters, but I couldn't say for sure." I glanced at Olivia. "I'm sorry."

She rubbed my arm gently. "It's all right."

"You need to let the two that I recognized go, at least," I begged.

"I'll see what I can do," Lisa promised.

"Can I see Daddy now?" I rasped.

"Yes, and then I'll need to ask you some questions."

"Perhaps you could ask those questions at her home," Olivia suggested. "Tomorrow."

"We need to speak today."

"It's okay, Olivia," I whispered. "Lisa, I left my phone at the church. Can someone call Jasmine or Parker, please?"

"Sure."

I pulled the leather jacket closer to my body, needing the comfort it was providing, and took a deep breath, drawing in the scent of leather and soap. Olivia helped me stand again, and we headed toward the door...just as

Hatch stalked in looking like he might kill someone.

"Yeah, thanks for nothin' asshole," an angry voice growled.

I turned toward the sound and saw Dash walking out from behind the secure doors.

"Where's Badger?" he snapped.

An officer frowned at him. "He's being processed."

"He was with me, fucker!"

"Sir. You need to calm down or I'm putting you back in a cell."

"Dash," Hatch called.

Dash spun on his heels and stalled, jabbing a finger at me as he approached. "What the fuck are you doing here?"

"She came to get you out," Hatch said.

"What?"

"Willow came down here, instead of going to see her dead father because she wanted to make sure you didn't rot in a jail cell," Olivia provided.

Dash studied me for a few tense seconds before letting out a sigh. "And the reason you're wearin' my jacket?"

"This is yours?" I asked.

"Yeah, babe, it is."

I moved to take off the jacket, but Olivia stopped me. "Dash doesn't need his jacket right now. Do you, Dash?"

"No. It's good," he said, and finally looked away from me. "They're not letting the other guys out," he said to Hatch.

"Yeah, guessed that," Hatch said. "Texted Mack."

"Good." Dash looked back to me, his expression softening. "You need to see your dad."

I forced back tears and nodded.

"I'm gonna come with you, okay?" he said.

I nodded again, feeling somewhat comforted by his presence. After the other man I'd identified came through security, we all piled into Hatch's rental car (me in the middle of the backseat), and headed to the coroner's office.

FOUR

Dash

PULLING UP TO the non-descript brick building, I climbed out of the car and leaned in to help Willow. She was shaky and I wasn't sure if it was from the meds or the shock…or both, but when she gripped my arm, I steadied her as we made our way inside.

When Olivia moved to take my place, I shook my head. I was already here and I wasn't about to leave her side. I was pissed they'd let her come down to the pig sty, but it was done and I couldn't change the past, so for now, I'd do everything I could to make sure she was supported.

"My name's Willow Miller," she said in a sad, quiet voice. "I think my father, Alfred, was brought here."

The older woman behind the counter stood, laying her

hand on Willow's, and gave her a gentle smile. "I'll just go and check, honey."

Willow nodded and I slid an arm around her waist when she leaned heavily against me. "I've got you."

"I can't do this," she whispered.

"You can," I assured her. "I'll be with you the whole way, yeah?"

She glanced at me with watery eyes and nodded. "Okay."

I gave her a gentle squeeze, my need to calm and protect this tiny slip of a woman surprising, even to myself.

The receptionist returned and ushered us into the back. The medical examiner introduced himself and I held Willow tighter when she began to shake.

"You're okay," I whispered.

"I'm going to let you see him, Miss Miller," the coroner said. "But you cannot touch him, do you understand?"

"I understand," she whispered.

The doctor pulled the sheet back and Willow crumpled. I held her up, turning her into my body and stroking her hair as she sobbed into my chest. "Daddy."

"That's him," I said.

"If you will leave your details with Sally at the front desk, she'll contact you when we're clear to release the body. She can also give you the details of the funeral homes we are familiar with."

Willow sobbed harder, but I held her close and nodded to the doctor. "Thanks, Doc." I slid my hand to her neck and cupped it. "Let's get out of here, okay? We'll figure it out."

She nodded and I half-carried her out of the cold, sterile room, and back to the lobby.

"Ohmigod, Willow!" a female voice cried.

"Jazz." She pulled away from me and walked into her friend's arms.

"I heard there was a shooting on the news and I've

been trying to call you for hours."

"I lost my phone," Willow rasped.

"Lisa called me and told me you were here."

"My dad's dead, Jasmine."

"I know, honey." She rubbed Willow's back. "Let's get you home, okay?"

Willow turned toward the reception desk. "I'm supposed to—"

"I'll get the information," I said. "I'll drop it by your house."

She met my eyes. "You don't know where I live."

"I'll find you."

She studied me for a few seconds and then let her friend walk her out of the building…still wearing my jacket.

* * *

Willow

JASMINE DROVE ME home and we had to hunt for the spare key because my purse was still at the church. I had nothing. No way to contact anyone or even get into my stupid house.

Once inside, I pulled Dash's jacket closer, still not wanting to take it off, the scent of him calming me. I settled myself on the sofa in the family room and stared at the ceiling.

"I left Brad a message," Jasmine said, sitting beside me and handing me a glass of water. "Hopefully, he'll call me back soon."

I realized in that moment I hadn't thought about him once. I'd had the worst thing in the world happen to me and he wasn't even on my radar. I glanced at my engagement ring and it was suddenly heavy on my hand.

"Parker's leaving work now and should be here in a few minutes."

"Thanks, Jazz," I said, and took a sip of water.

"Who were the people with you at the coroner's office?"

"Bikers." I gasped. "Oh, my word. I didn't even thank them."

"I'm sure they understand."

I bit my lip. "My dad told me to run...to get help. The closest place is Barney's." I blinked back tears. "He won't be happy with me for going there. I mean...oh! He's gone, Jazz." I burst into tears again and Jasmine pulled me close, bumping my arm which made me squeak in pain.

"Willow?"

"I was shot."

"Holy shit!" she snapped. "You were *shot*? Why didn't you tell me? Why aren't you in the hospital? Where?"

Jasmine was one of my "low-class" friends according to Brad. She drank, she swore, and she told it like it was. She was a human mirror and that was awesome when you liked what you saw, but if you didn't, she bristled people...people like Brad. But I loved her more than life itself. She always told me the truth, even if it was hard to hear, and she would die for me.

Parker was just as loyal, only in a quieter way. She was Brad-approved, but that was only because she was rich and had been raised the "right way." My dad had loved both of them and I now clung to that fact as Jasmine fussed over me.

"Doc sewed me up and gave me something for the pain, but it's wearing off." I slid my right arm out of the jacket and Jasmine examined it.

"Who the hell is Doc?" she demanded.

"He was there with Olivia and Hatch...and Dash."

"Dash?"

"The man who..." I swallowed. "At the coroner's."

"The one who belongs to this jacket."

I nodded and slipped my arm back in, once again feeling safe. "Yes."

"I think you might want to take it off before Brad gets here," she warned.

I shook my head. I couldn't yet. In the few hours I'd been wearing it, I'd come to rely on its comfort.

"Okay, honey. Let me call my dad. See if he can get you something for the pain."

Jasmine's dad was a doctor and had his general practice in downtown Savannah. He'd been a Godsend when my mother was battling cancer, and was like a second father to me.

"Willow? Jazz?" Parker called, letting herself into the house.

"Back here," Jasmine called as she pulled her phone out of her purse.

The next four hours could only be described as controlled chaos. Jasmine played host as people from the church brought food and flowers, and then refereed when they wanted to sit down and tell me how wonderful my father was and how much he'd be missed. She and Parker helped to usher those who wanted to stay too long out of the house without hurting anyone's feelings.

Jasmine's father had arrived an hour into the mayhem with a prescription of Percocet and something to help me sleep. He'd also brought a bag for Jasmine who'd declared she'd be staying with me for a few days.

Brad still hadn't come. He hadn't called either and this bothered me, but it was also a relief. There was really only one person I wanted to see and he belonged to the leather now engulfing me.

The doorbell rang a few minutes after the last person left and I groaned. "I can't visit anymore."

"I'll get rid of them," Jasmine offered, and made her way to the front door.

Heavy booted footsteps sounded on the hardwoods and I rolled my head to see Dash walk into the room. Goodness, he was handsome. Something I really shouldn't notice, but I couldn't help myself. Dark hair that fell over his forehead, deep blue eyes, and muscles upon muscles, clearly showcased by his white T-shirt. He was lean, but probably because he was so tall. Close to a foot taller than me.

"Hi." I rose to my shaky feet, but he shook his head.

"Hey," he said. "Sit down."

I sat down and pulled his jacket close again. Dash smiled gently and handed me a phone. "Burner to hold you over until you get yours back. Programmed a couple numbers in there in case you need one of us."

"Thank you. That's really sweet."

Jasmine and Parker shared a "look," but I ignored them. We could debrief later. I nodded to the chair next to me and Dash pulled a piece of paper out of his pocket, then took his seat. "Got all the information about funeral homes and that kind of shit." He handed it to me. "But you don't need to do anything today."

"Okay, thanks." I took a deep breath.

"Still wearin' my jacket, I see."

I nodded. "Is that okay?"

"Yeah, babe, it's all good."

"I can't believe you found me."

He chuckled. "Yeah, took a minute. You're not listed, and this might be a small town, but it's tight-lipped when it comes to you."

I sighed. "I know. Dad wanted me safe."

"Good man."

I met his eyes. "He really was." I burst into tears again, dropping my face into my hands. "I don't know what I'm going to do without him."

I felt the sofa dip and then strong arms guided me against a very familiar chest. "I got you."

I buried my face into his T-shirt and sobbed until I felt like I had nothing left. "I'm sorry," I rasped. "I keep soaking your T-shirt."

He chuckled. "It's all good, Willow. I've got several."

I smoothed my hand down his chest, over the area I'd crumpled with my fist. He laid his hand over mine and gave it a squeeze before guiding it away from his body. I suddenly felt mortified that I'd touched him so intimately and felt the heat flood my face. "Sorry."

"All good, babe." He rose to his feet. "I should get goin'."

My heart suddenly raced. I didn't want him to go, but I forced my panic aside and nodded.

He raised an eyebrow. "You need to keep my jacket for a bit?"

"Oh, right." I bit my lip as I stood. "Um..."

"I can pick it up in a couple days."

"Won't you need it?"

"You like it?"

I sighed. "It makes me feel safe," I blurted.

He stroked my cheek. "I'll pick it up in a couple of days."

I swallowed as I leaned into his hand. "Thank you."

"You need me, you call, yeah? You get scared, you call. You want to cry, you call."

I nodded. "Okay."

"Okay." He smiled, then walked out of the room and I heard the front door close then the roar of motorcycle pipes.

"What the hell was *that*?" Jasmine demanded, forcing me to sit down again.

Parker sat in the chair Dash had been in earlier and stared at me in her quiet, disconcerting way.

I filled them in on Dash's incarceration and his help at the coroner identifying my father's body, but I left out everything that happened at the church. I wasn't ready to talk about it. I wasn't sure if I'd ever be, but for the moment, they gave me space.

"He's really hot," Parker whispered, and Jasmine choked.

"I'm sorry?" she said.

"Well, he is," Parker pressed.

The new topic of conversation brought a small levity to my day and I was able to genuinely smile. "Not that I would admit noticing, but I'd have to agree. He was also very kind to me even though I got him thrown into jail."

"Technically, you didn't get him thrown into jail, Willow," Jasmine countered.

"No, but if he hadn't been helping me, he wouldn't have had to deal with any of that, and some of his friends are still in there." I sighed. "I should have just called the police, but I wasn't really thinking straight."

"It's okay, Willow," Parker assured me. "I'm sure they'll figure it out."

"Can you ask Levi to help?"

Parker's brother, Levi, was an attorney, and although he specialized in environmental law, he was the only lawyer I knew, so I had to ask.

Parker smiled. "I'll call him right now."

"Thanks."

"Any word from Brad?" Parker asked Jasmine.

"Nothing yet," she said, and I could tell she was trying to hold back her irritation…not well, but she was trying.

I yawned and sank further into the sofa.

"Maybe you should rest," Parker said.

"I'm fine here," I said. I wasn't ready to go upstairs. Upstairs was where my dad's room was. I couldn't go there yet.

"Stretch out, honey," Jasmine ordered. "Sleep."

I nodded and settled myself on the side that wasn't stitched up, letting the pain meds do their thing and succumbing to a fitful sleep.

* * *

Dash

FUCK ME, WHAT the hell had I just gotten myself into? When I'd walked into her house, and she was still wearing my fuckin' jacket, I had to stop myself from pulling her into a room and kissing her 'til she came.

Then, when she cried into my chest and ran her tiny hand over my stomach, I thought I might fuckin' come myself. I had no business sniffin' around a preacher's daughter, but even though I knew that, I also knew I wouldn't stay away. She looked good in my patch. Like it was right where it should be.

I pulled my bike up to the compound and backed it into a parking space, then headed inside. I was grateful for the warmth of the building...I was fuckin' cold, and knew I'd need to grab another jacket before the sun went down.

"Dash!" Hatch called from his place at the bar.

"Hey," I greeted, and walked their way.

"How's Willow?" he asked.

"Fuckin' sad."

Hatch nodded. "She got people?"

"Two of her friends were there when I got there. I think she's good."

"See you didn't get your jacket back," Hatch said.

"Nope." I grabbed a beer and twisted off the top.

Hatch chuckled, but I ignored him. He obviously knew I'd had no power over Willow keepin' my jacket, but didn't press me on the subject. Smart man.

"Any word on Badger and the guys?" I asked, then took a swig of beer.

"Got a call in to Mack. He's got some contacts here, but he's gonna try and fly out this week."

Mack Reed was one of the officer's in the Portland chapter and was also a really good attorney. We didn't yet have access to someone like him here, so it was good he was willing to travel at a moment's notice. Rusty, the bartender, had also been released and he'd texted me to let me know the other guy workin' the bar had been let out, but none of the Dogs, which led me to believe there was an agenda when it came to our club.

"Fuck!" I hissed. "It's that damn sheriff. He's such an asshole."

"Seems like it," Hatch said.

"He's been gunnin' for us for years," Doc said, approaching from the back patio. "He can't hold 'em for much longer without arrestin' them, though. And he can't arrest 'em without evidence."

"Wouldn't put it past him to 'find' some," I ground out.

"True," he said, sounding defeated. "You see the girl?"

"Yeah, man."

"She okay?"

"Define okay," I said.

"Her arm okay? Is she in pain?"

"She seemed good on that front," I said.

"She still got your jacket?"

"Shut up," I retorted, and saw Doc give Hatch a grin.

I ignored their silent ribbing and finished my beer. As the night wore on, women approached, some I'd had before, some I hadn't, but I turned them down. I couldn't get Willow out of my head and the thought of fuckin' some random gash turned my stomach. Instead, I headed to my room hours earlier than I normally would have.

Dash

FUCK ME, WHAT the hell had I just gotten myself into? When I'd walked into her house, and she was still wearing my fuckin' jacket, I had to stop myself from pulling her into a room and kissing her 'til she came.

Then, when she cried into my chest and ran her tiny hand over my stomach, I thought I might fuckin' come myself. I had no business sniffin' around a preacher's daughter, but even though I knew that, I also knew I wouldn't stay away. She looked good in my patch. Like it was right where it should be.

I pulled my bike up to the compound and backed it into a parking space, then headed inside. I was grateful for the warmth of the building…I was fuckin' cold, and knew I'd need to grab another jacket before the sun went down.

"Dash!" Hatch called from his place at the bar.

"Hey," I greeted, and walked their way.

"How's Willow?" he asked.

"Fuckin' sad."

Hatch nodded. "She got people?"

"Two of her friends were there when I got there. I think she's good."

"See you didn't get your jacket back," Hatch said.

"Nope." I grabbed a beer and twisted off the top.

Hatch chuckled, but I ignored him. He obviously knew I'd had no power over Willow keepin' my jacket, but didn't press me on the subject. Smart man.

"Any word on Badger and the guys?" I asked, then took a swig of beer.

"Got a call in to Mack. He's got some contacts here, but he's gonna try and fly out this week."

Mack Reed was one of the officer's in the Portland chapter and was also a really good attorney. We didn't yet have access to someone like him here, so it was good he was willing to travel at a moment's notice. Rusty, the bartender, had also been released and he'd texted me to let me know the other guy workin' the bar had been let out, but none of the Dogs, which led me to believe there was an agenda when it came to our club.

"Fuck!" I hissed. "It's that damn sheriff. He's such an asshole."

"Seems like it," Hatch said.

"He's been gunnin' for us for years," Doc said, approaching from the back patio. "He can't hold 'em for much longer without arrestin' them, though. And he can't arrest 'em without evidence."

"Wouldn't put it past him to 'find' some," I ground out.

"True," he said, sounding defeated. "You see the girl?"

"Yeah, man."

"She okay?"

"Define okay," I said.

"Her arm okay? Is she in pain?"

"She seemed good on that front," I said.

"She still got your jacket?"

"Shut up," I retorted, and saw Doc give Hatch a grin.

I ignored their silent ribbing and finished my beer. As the night wore on, women approached, some I'd had before, some I hadn't, but I turned them down. I couldn't get Willow out of my head and the thought of fuckin' some random gash turned my stomach. Instead, I headed to my room hours earlier than I normally would have.

FIVE

Willow

THE SOUND OF screaming and the coppery smell of blood shook me awake, and for several seconds, I had no idea where I was, but my heart was racing and I felt sick to my stomach.

I sat up and blindly reached for something...anything... my hand connecting with my security blanket of late. I pulled the jacket close to my chest and took a deep breath. The smell of leather and Dash's intoxicating scent gave me instant comfort.

I thought about Dash and the sweetness he'd shown, in vast contrast to that of my fiancé. Brad had never come by. Oh, he'd called to check on me and make sure I was okay, but he'd been too busy to come to the house and offer any comfort.

A virtual stranger, however, had taken the time to rush into a dangerous situation, get himself arrested, then still offer me support when I had to identify my father. This so-called 'degenerate' had shown me more care and tenderness than my 'upstanding' and 'good' fiancé. I was a little over it.

I reached for the phone on my nightstand, grimacing as I pulled the stitches in my arm a little. Checking the time, I debated on calling him, but he'd said I could, so I did.

"Yeah?" a sleepy voice answered.

"Uh, sorry, were you sleeping?"

"Yeah, babe. You okay?"

"Bad dreams."

"Yeah?"

"Yes," I whispered. "Sorry, I shouldn't bother you, but…"

"It's all good, Willow. I told you to call."

"I know, but you don't know me and I don't want to take advantage of your kindness," I said. "I just can't get the sounds out of my head."

"You wanna talk about it?"

"I don't know," I admitted. "But I'm supposed to give a statement tomorrow and I'm not sure I can."

"Might help to talk it out first."

"Maybe." Good Lord, this man was sweet. "My dad's lawyer called after you left."

"Yeah?"

"I didn't even know he had a lawyer…I mean, one that wasn't affiliated with the church."

"What did he say?"

"That my dad left everything to me and I could pick up the paperwork anytime."

"Paperwork?" he asked.

"A full list of his assets and things like that."

"Makes sense."

I sat up slightly and sighed. "I'm pretty sure the house is mortgaged heavily, so I'm not sure I'd call it an asset."

"I guess you'll know when the lawyer walks you through everything."

"Yeah," I said, laying back on the pillows. "I'm really sorry I woke you."

"It's fine, Willow. Stop apologizin'."

"Why are you being so nice?"

"Because I'm nice."

I smiled. "This is true."

He chuckled. "I'd think, bein' a preacher's daughter, you'd be used to nice."

"I am, but I'm also used to people pretending to be nice in God's name," I admitted.

"Yeah?"

"Unfortunately, yes."

"That sucks."

"Yes, it does." I sighed. "Why are you called Dash?"

"Right to the heart of it, huh?"

"Sorry, is that too personal?"

"No. But that's for another day."

I wrinkled my nose. "Oh, okay."

"How's your arm?" he asked.

"It hurts." I grimaced. "I should take another pill, but I'm afraid to fall asleep again."

"You got someone staying with you?"

"Yes. Jazz is here."

"Any issues?"

"You mean other than the nightmares?"

"Yeah."

"No. The house is locked up tight, we have food for days…lots of people came by and dropped off meals…I have carrot and raisin salad up the wazoo."

He chuckled. "Sounds disgustin'."

"It is. I have never met anyone who eats it, so I don't understand why people continue to make it…and in so much abundance." I sighed. "I can't believe I'm talking to you about carrot salad."

"You avoidin' talkin' about somethin' else?"

"Probably," I answered immediately.

"You know it's okay if you don't want to talk about it, Willow. You don't have to."

"I'll have to tomorrow."

"Want me to come with you?"

"It's at the police station."

"Yeah, Willow, I figured that."

I bit back tears. "You'd come with me?"

"Do you want me to?"

"Kind of, yes."

"Then I'll come."

"Gosh, you are *so* nice," I breathed out.

"Am I?"

"*Yes*," I insisted. "My fiancé should be coming with me."

"You got a fiancé?" he asked, his voice quiet and sounding a little irritated.

"Sort of."

"How do you 'sort of' have a fiancé, Willow?"

I have no idea why I did it, but I suddenly gave him a blow-by-blow of my entire relationship with Brad. Everything, even things that irritated me, but I'd brushed off previously. And the more I talked, the more I realized I didn't want to marry Brad. I didn't even want to date him.

"Sounds like a douche."

"I don't think I want to be that cruel, because I thought I loved him at one point, but now I don't think I do," I said. "He hasn't shown much kindness over the last twenty-four hours and I'm kind of over it."

"I think you're bein' gracious."

"Maybe so," I conceded. "What did you do after you left my house?"

"Went back to the club and had a beer. Hatch is worried about you."

"He is?"

"Yeah."

"He's so nice," I said. "Did he tell you I met him when I was little?"

"Nope."

"He was nice then, too. Actually, all y'all are really nice."

"And that surprises you?"

"Yes," I admitted. "I hate that it does, but I was always warned to stay away from the biker bar. My dad wouldn't even let me drive past it."

"What made you run there then?"

"I'm not sure really. I guess I knew exactly where it was, and that I could take cover in the thick trees in case anyone was watching."

"Smart girl."

The compliment warmed me in a weird way. "Can I tell you something Dash?"

"Of course, anything."

"I could see everything through the slats of the closet," I whispered.

"Yeah?" he said quietly like he didn't want to spook me.

"They came in and demanded money from my dad. They wore ski masks, but one of the men's voices was different."

"Different how?"

"Appalachian almost, but he had a lisp."

"That's good, Willow. That's a clue."

"I'm really sorry I couldn't say for sure I had seen your other friends in the bar. I would have if I could have, and I almost lied to get them out, but I've never been good at lying and I knew Lisa would be able to tell."

"It's okay, baby. We'll figure it out."

Him calling me 'baby' did things to me and I really

liked it...but I wasn't sure I was supposed to like it and I warred with that for a few seconds. "Parker's brother is a lawyer. She called him to see if he can help. Is it okay if I give him your number?"

"Yeah, that's cool. We've got a guy comin' out from Portland, but if you want to give him my number, it's fine."

"They shot him four times, Dash. Once in the knee, once in the arm, then in his stomach twice. When they shot him, a bullet went through the closet and hit me. I had to bite down on my hand not to scream."

"You did real good, Willow. If they'd found you, they might have killed you too."

"That's what my dad said," I whispered. "When they thought he was dead, he told me to run. I didn't want to leave him. I should have stayed and put pressure on his wounds or something."

"He was pretty far gone when I found him."

"*You* found him?"

"Yeah. I stayed with him until I was cuffed. Putting pressure on his wounds wouldn't have helped."

"Did he...did he say anything?"

"Yeah, but I want to tell you that face-to-face."

"But if you tell me face-to-face, I won't be able to control my emotions."

"That's okay, Willow. I want to be there to make sure you're okay," he said. "I don't want to tell you anything at three in the morning while you're in pain."

"That's probably smart." I squeezed my eyes shut. "Was he mad at me?"

"No...of course not. What the hell would he be mad at you about?"

"Nothing. I don't know. I always feel like I'm doing something wrong."

"Religious guilt."

I smiled. "You're probably right."

"I'm always right."

"Are you?" I deadpanned. "That's a pretty nifty trick."

"Man of many talents," he retorted. "What time do you need to be down at the station?"

"Eleven."

"I'll pick you up at ten-thirty."

"You really don't have to do that, Dash. I can get Jazz to drive me."

"I'll be there at ten-thirty," he said in a tone that broached no argument.

"Okay," I said. "Thanks for letting me vent."

"No problem," he said. "You feel better?"

"I still don't want to go back to sleep, but yes."

"I'll stay on the line with you until you do, but I want you to take some meds."

"Yes, sir." I sat up and opened the pill bottle. "So serious."

"No one's ever accused me of being 'so serious' before," he said, and I could hear the smile in his voice.

"Then they must not know you." I popped a pill and swallowed it with some water.

He chuckled. "Couple hours of crying on my shirt and you know me better than anyone, huh?"

I bit my lip. "I didn't mean—"

"It's all good, Willow. I'm messin' with ya."

"I'll need to get used to that. Jazz is the only one who's sarcastic with me...the Bible says it's a sin."

"Does it?"

"In a roundabout way, yes."

"Well, then I'm fuckin' goin' straight to hell."

"Don't say that," I whispered. I'd been raised to believe if you speak it, it will happen. I never fully held to that belief, but the thought of Dash going to hell didn't sit well with me and I didn't want him to say things like that...just in case.

"Babe, I'm not goin' to hell. God has already sent me

to Bakersfield twice, so technically he still owes me."

I giggled. "I hope not, but just do me a favor and keep those thoughts to yourself."

"I like that you're worried about my eternal damnation, baby."

"I'm worried about *everyone's* eternal damnation," I retorted.

"Fair enough."

"Can I ask you a question?"

"What are you doing right now?"

I rolled my eyes. "Do you call everyone 'baby'?"

"Never called a man 'baby.'"

"But do you say that to every woman?"

He sighed, but didn't speak for several tense seconds. "No, Willow, I don't call every woman 'baby.' You're the first."

"Wow," I whispered.

"You good?"

"Yes."

"I'll be at your place at ten-thirty."

"Okay," I said, pulling the jacket closer to me. "Dash?"

"Yeah, Willow?"

"Thank you. For everything."

"You're welcome."

I snuggled further into his jacket. "I'll see you tomorrow."

"Night."

I hung up wishing he'd called me baby again, but still falling asleep with a smile on my face.

* * *

Dash

I DROPPED MY cell phone onto the nightstand and dragged my hands down my face. Goddammit! Engaged. I should walk away. Fuck that. I should *run*.

I should, but I knew I wouldn't. In a matter of hours, this beautiful, innocent, and sweet-as-fuck preacher's daughter had wormed her way into my heart. I didn't know how, sure as hell didn't want it, but regardless, it had happened.

I'd never called a woman 'baby.' Believed it was for someone I cared about. I'd never talked to one for over an hour on the phone either. And sure as hell not at three in the morning. Willow was makin' me do things I'd never done before, and I didn't care. I liked the way she made me feel, and welcomed the change.

I dragged myself out of my bed at the compound and hit the head. Falling back into bed, it took me a while to get back to sleep, my thoughts filled with Willow and what I planned to do to her once I got her naked and under me.

Awoken by my phone buzzing again, I answered it expecting Willow. It wasn't.

"Brother, it's Doc."

"What's wrong?"

"Mack's here. You need to fill him in on everything."

I glanced at the clock. Nine. Gave me about an hour to tell him what I knew. I sighed. "I'll be down in ten."

"Okay, man."

Doc hung up and I showered quickly, then headed downstairs. Mack and Doc were in the kitchen, pouring coffee, so I grabbed a mug and did the same.

"Hey, man," Mack said, and shook my hand.

"Hey. You bring Darien?"

"Nah. She's got shit goin' on with the movie and takin' care of the kids."

Mack and Darien had two kids now, and she was a best-selling romance author, whose books were being turned into movies. They were currently filming in Portland, and several of us had wanted to head out for the chance to meet the movie's star, pop princess-turned actress, Melody Morgan.

"Was it tough to get a flight?" I asked.

Mack chuckled. "Guess who flew private?"

"Yeah?" Doc asked.

"Yeah. RatHound loaned me their plane."

I choked on my coffee. "What the fuck?"

"Seriously?" Doc asked. "You know RatHound?"

"Do you also hang out with Springsteen too?"

"Long story," Mack said. "I'll fill you in another time."

I nodded.

"You good to talk for a bit?" Mack asked.

"Yeah." I glanced at my watch. "Gotta leave here around ten-fifteen, but can fill you in on what I know."

Mack nodded, and we headed to one of the private offices in the back.

"You alright?" he asked, sounding genuinely concerned.

"I'm good, just pissed."

"Good, I'm glad you're okay," he said, his tone changing sharply. "Because I'm also fuckin' pissed! What the fuck were you idiots thinking?"

"What?" I snapped. "What the fuck were we supposed to do? Doc was there when I rounded up the crew."

"Did he know you were going in heavy?"

"Heavy? Jesus, man, you make it sound like we rolled up, looking for a gun fight."

"Watch it, pup. The stitches on your patch are a little too fresh for that kind of tone with me."

"The stitches may be fresh, but they still hold up a full patch. You know I respect you, Mack, but what the fuck were we supposed to do? All we knew was there was a girl, she was shot, and her dad was in trouble. Of course we went in armed. Don't tell me you wouldn't have too."

"Don't presume to think you have a goddamned clue what I would have done. This is the kind of disrespectful shit I'm talking about." He stared at me silently for a few moments before continuing, "You're a good guy, Dash. A good guy, with a big heart."

"Thanks."

"Don't thank me. 'Cause that big heart of yours, coupled with that big mouth, is gonna get you thrown in prison again…or killed. Shut up and do what I tell you to do, if you want to get out of this."

"Out of what? I haven't done anything wrong. The cops let me go, and Willow told them I didn't have anything to do with the shooting."

"That's all true, but the Sheriff and the D.A. still want to know why there were a bunch of bikers running around the church with guns at the time of a mass shooting."

"All I know is that we went in, saw the receptionist on the floor, checked for a pulse and then I saw Willow's dad. Before I knew what was happening, the cops were on us like flies on shit. Deputy Bettincourt, this asshole we all went to high school with, took our guns and we were off to the station."

"Did they read you your rights?" Mack asked.

"They barely said shit to us, and we didn't resist. Once we got to the station, we were told we were being held on the suspicion of murder. Not long after Willow showed up, and since she could ID me and provide me with an alibi, they let me go."

"They can only hold the others for seventy-two hours without charging them, so we should know soon what they plan on doing."

"Those asshole cops know the club didn't do shit. They're just lookin' for a reason to jam us up!" I snapped.

"Well you made their jobs pretty fucking easy, showing up to the scene of a mass shooting, armed for World War III," Mack grumbled.

"What the hell are you talking about? I had my Glock, Badger had his .38, and we both have our concealed carry permits. I'm sure Fletch and Gator were packing, but it's not like we rolled up in a tank or anything."

"What about the Raptors' guys?"

"What about 'em?"

"Those guys are known to carry some pretty heavy artillery, and from what I understand it's not always exactly clean."

I dragged my hands down my face. "I didn't exactly take weapons inventory before we left the bar, Mack. What the fuck do you want from me?"

"I want you to think a little more before you bring any more heat on the club."

"The cops know we didn't have anything to do with this, and they're gonna have to let everyone else out soon, you said so yourself."

"Maybe, but any potential weapons charges associated with this club are going to be a big fucking hassle for all of us." He looked at me even more seriously. "And a big fucking deal to the Prez."

I sighed. It was what it was and there was nothing I could do about it, so I had to wait it out and let Mack do his worst. I had a woman to take care of, and right now, she was the priority.

SIX

Willow

HE WAS LATE. Granted, he was only ten minutes late and we were only fifteen minutes from the station, but still, I felt a little sick. Maybe he'd changed his mind. Maybe he wasn't coming at all.

Jazz was in the shower, so I flopped onto the sofa and turned on the television. I'd avoided any kind of media coverage, mostly because Jazz and Parker had played referee. I didn't mind at the time, but now I felt out of the loop, so I flipped to the local news channel…and immediately wished I hadn't.

"Hi, folks. If you're just joining us, we're updating you on the First Baptist Church massacre. We have confirmed *there were four people killed, including a twelve-year-old girl..."*

I swallowed down bile. The only kid I'd seen before the shooting started was Eleanor's daughter, Taylor. I felt tears stream down my face as the reporter listed the other fatalities. I knew them all.

"Willow Annabelle Miller," Jasmine snapped, rushing to me and grabbing the remote, flipping it off.

"Why didn't you tell me?" I ground out.

"Because you were in pain and when you weren't in pain, you were hopped up on meds or sedated."

"Was it Taylor?"

"Yeah, honey," Jasmine said. "She came running when she heard her mom scream and they took her out."

"Oh, my word," I sobbed.

Jasmine wrapped an arm around my shoulders and gave me a gentle hug. "You need to take a minute. It's okay. It's all going to be okay."

Before I could comment, the doorbell rang and Jasmine went to answer the door. Finally, Dash was here to make me feel better.

Only it wasn't Dash.

"Hello, sweetheart," Brad said, and sat beside me on the sofa.

"Hi, Brad."

He took my hand and shifted to face me. "You've been crying again."

"Yeah, that happens when your father's killed in front of you," Jasmine ground out.

He didn't pull me against his chest and hold me, he chastely held my hand as though I was no more than a neighbor or a friend. I pulled my hand away from his.

"Where's your ring?" he asked.

I rose to my feet and grabbed it from the kitchen, handing it to him.

"Why is it not on your finger?" he demanded.

"I'm sorry, Brad, but I think we should rethink our engagement."

I heard Jasmine make a quiet squeak and then she walked out of the room.

"Willow," Brad said slowly. "Sweetheart, you've had a shock."

"Exactly. And this is the first time I'm seeing you."

He sighed. "I was extremely busy. I tried to break away, I really did."

"But you didn't." I sat back down. "I would think, as your fiancée, that you'd just make it happen!"

"It doesn't work that way, Willow."

"Surely, your boss wouldn't have a problem with you rushing to comfort your grieving fiancée."

"We have a very important deadline, sweetheart, that was my priority."

"Well, I don't want to be second anymore, Brad."

"After all the time and effort I've put in to get you ready for politics?" he snapped.

"I'm sorry?" I asked, my mouth dropping open in shock.

"Years, Willow. I have been working to get you up to par."

"Up to par?" I snapped. "I thought you proposed because you loved me, but you're telling me I was your *project?*"

"Don't be naïve, Willow. You knew exactly what this was."

"Is there a problem here?" a deep voice demanded.

I turned to see Dash walking into the room, irritation etched in the tight expression of his face.

"Who are you?" Brad demanded.

"Who the fuck are you?" he spit back.

My heart raced as Dash stepped in front of me and stood toe-to-toe with Brad.

Brad scowled. "I'm Willow's fiancé."

"Not anymore, you're not," I corrected.

Dash glanced at me over his shoulder, but didn't respond to my announcement.

"Since when do you hang around with low-lifes?" Brad challenged.

"The only low-life I see here is you, dickhead," Jasmine hissed.

"You always were a bitch, Jazz," he said.

"Don't talk to her that way!" I demanded.

"I think it would be good for you to go, asshole," Dash said.

Brad jabbed a finger toward me. "This conversation isn't over."

"Yes, it is," I breathed out in frustration.

Dash stepped closer to me as Brad tried to reach for me. "Not gonna happen," he growled.

I laid my hand on his back, drawing in his strength.

"I'll call you in a day or two," Brad countered. "Or you can call me anytime…when you come to your senses."

"Don't hold your breath," I retorted, and with one final scowl, he stalked out of the house.

Jasmine followed him, probably to make sure she locked the door, and Dash faced me. "You cryin' because of him?"

I shook my head. "No, having him out of my life is a welcomed relief right now."

His face softened and he wiped a tear away. "Did somethin' happen, Willow?"

"I watched the news."

He sighed, pulling me close. "So, you found out more than maybe you should have?"

I dropped my head to his chest. "A little girl died, Dash."

"I know, baby." He slid his hand to my hair and stroked it.

"Taylor was the sweetest person on earth," I continued. "Not a mean bone in her body and was watching the little kids so their parents could worship and do a Bible study without interruption. She was checking on her Mama and was killed because of it. It's not fair."

"I know," he whispered.

"Sam's lost his wife *and* his baby. Who can survive that?" I gripped his shirt. "Why would God let this happen? All those people…just visiting and spending time in God's house. Why, Dash?"

He didn't say anything. Just continued to hold me while I raged and sobbed and raged some more.

I felt him shift, but kept his arms around me as he guided me to the sofa and pulled me onto his lap. I burrowed against his body and he held me tight again, letting me cry everything out.

"I'm going to call the station," Jasmine said. "Today's just not a good day."

"No, it's okay," I said. "Dash came all the way—"

"Call the station," Dash said, interrupting me.

"You wasted all this time—"

He squeezed my neck. "Babe, it's all good."

I met his eyes. "Are you sure?"

"Yeah, Willow, I'm sure."

"Don't you have a job?"

He chuckled. "Yeah, baby, but it's flexible."

"*This* flexible?"

"Yeah, Willow. *This* flexible."

"I don't want to keep you from your life," I pressed. "Please don't feel like you need to hang around."

"Do you want me to go?"

"No," I answered immediately. "But you can if you need to."

"I'm good right here," he said.

"Can you stay for a while?" Jasmine asked from the kitchen.

Dash craned his head to see her. "Yeah. You need to be somewhere?"

"Yes. But only if Willow won't be alone."

He nodded. "My guys know I'm out of pocket for a while."

"I'm sorry I've taken up all your time, Jazz," I said.

Jasmine smiled. "Don't even worry about it. I just need to run home and check on Scruffy and return some emails, but I can be back before dinner."

Scruffy was Jasmine's very obnoxious cat, and even if he hadn't been obnoxious, I still wouldn't be able to tolerate him with my allergies. Luckily, I didn't have to insult her satanic little 'precious,' using my allergies as a very valid reason not to be in his presence.

I focused back on Dash. "You sure you're okay to stay? I can call Parker."

He smiled. "I'm good."

I suddenly realized I was sitting on his lap and could feel the heat creep up my face. As I moved to climb off of him, he held tight. "Where ya goin?"

"I...ah..."

"You shy, Willow?"

"No," I said. "But I have never sat on a man's lap before...I mean, as an adult."

"What a coincidence, neither have I."

I giggled. "It's kind of nice. You should try it."

"I like that sound."

I took a deep breath. "I like making it."

"Do me a favor."

"Okay," I promised carefully.

"No more news for a while."

"I can do that," I promised. "But I should really check on those families."

"It can wait."

"They might need someone to talk to."

"You lost your dad, Willow. It. Can. Wait," he

"Taylor was the sweetest person on earth," I continued. "Not a mean bone in her body and was watching the little kids so their parents could worship and do a Bible study without interruption. She was checking on her Mama and was killed because of it. It's not fair."

"I know," he whispered.

"Sam's lost his wife *and* his baby. Who can survive that?" I gripped his shirt. "Why would God let this happen? All those people…just visiting and spending time in God's house. Why, Dash?"

He didn't say anything. Just continued to hold me while I raged and sobbed and raged some more.

I felt him shift, but kept his arms around me as he guided me to the sofa and pulled me onto his lap. I burrowed against his body and he held me tight again, letting me cry everything out.

"I'm going to call the station," Jasmine said. "Today's just not a good day."

"No, it's okay," I said. "Dash came all the way—"

"Call the station," Dash said, interrupting me.

"You wasted all this time—"

He squeezed my neck. "Babe, it's all good."

I met his eyes. "Are you sure?"

"Yeah, Willow, I'm sure."

"Don't you have a job?"

He chuckled. "Yeah, baby, but it's flexible."

"*This* flexible?"

"Yeah, Willow. *This* flexible."

"I don't want to keep you from your life," I pressed. "Please don't feel like you need to hang around."

"Do you want me to go?"

"No," I answered immediately. "But you can if you need to."

"I'm good right here," he said.

"Can you stay for a while?" Jasmine asked from the kitchen.

Dash craned his head to see her. "Yeah. You need to be somewhere?"

"Yes. But only if Willow won't be alone."

He nodded. "My guys know I'm out of pocket for a while."

"I'm sorry I've taken up all your time, Jazz," I said.

Jasmine smiled. "Don't even worry about it. I just need to run home and check on Scruffy and return some emails, but I can be back before dinner."

Scruffy was Jasmine's very obnoxious cat, and even if he hadn't been obnoxious, I still wouldn't be able to tolerate him with my allergies. Luckily, I didn't have to insult her satanic little 'precious,' using my allergies as a very valid reason not to be in his presence.

I focused back on Dash. "You sure you're okay to stay? I can call Parker."

He smiled. "I'm good."

I suddenly realized I was sitting on his lap and could feel the heat creep up my face. As I moved to climb off of him, he held tight. "Where ya goin?"

"I…ah…"

"You shy, Willow?"

"No," I said. "But I have never sat on a man's lap before…I mean, as an adult."

"What a coincidence, neither have I."

I giggled. "It's kind of nice. You should try it."

"I like that sound."

I took a deep breath. "I like making it."

"Do me a favor."

"Okay," I promised carefully.

"No more news for a while."

"I can do that," I promised. "But I should really check on those families."

"It can wait."

"They might need someone to talk to."

"You lost your dad, Willow. It. Can. Wait," he

pressed.

I nodded and settled back against his chest. "Okay."

Jasmine walked over to us and leaned down to kiss my cheek. "I'll see you later. Don't get up...I'll lock up."

"Thanks, Jazz."

She waved a finger between us. "Not sure what this is, but I like it."

"Jazz!" I admonished, but Dash just chuckled.

She gave me a goofy grin and left us alone.

"Sorry about that," I said.

"Why are you sorry?"

"Because Jasmine's all heart and a total romantic." I smiled. "It's why she can't keep a man...she has way too many expectations on what she wants." I gasped. "I shouldn't have told you that." I sat up with a frown. "Why do I keep telling you everything? This is totally not like me."

"I'm not gonna tell anyone what you tell me," he said.

"I appreciate that, but I really shouldn't be sharing secrets that aren't my own." I scrambled off his lap.

He obviously wasn't prepared for my escape, because I was able to put distance between us. "Willow."

"What?" I asked as I escaped into the kitchen.

He stood and made his way to me, pinning me to the kitchen island and boxing me in with his arms. "Wanna know somethin'?"

I licked my lips. "What?" I squeaked.

"I'm also not sure what this is, but I like it too."

"You do?"

"Yeah, baby. I do." He smiled. "You scared?"

I shook my head.

He leaned closer. "You like this?"

I nodded.

His mouth covered mine and I gasped giving him better access to my mouth. His tongue swept inside and I grabbed his shirt to stay upright as he kissed me better than I'd ever been kissed in my life.

His hand went to my neck and he stroked my pulse as he deepened the kiss, while my heart felt like it would explode out of my chest. Lordy, this was good. So, so good.

Dash broke our connection and dropped his forehead to mine. "Wow."

I smiled and whispered, "Wow, indeed."

"You good with explorin' this?"

"I don't know."

"Why don't you know?"

I took a deep breath...then another. "Because you're forbidden."

"How so?"

"I was warned about bikers and I've seen enough cable TV to know our worlds couldn't be further apart."

"You think?"

"Yes," I said. "You are the second man I've ever kissed, and as much as I like the way you kiss the best, I'm not sure I'd be enough for you."

"Why wouldn't you be enough, Willow?"

I stared at his shirt.

"Look at me, baby."

I met his eyes and bit my lip. "I have never...um...you know."

"I don't know. Why don't you tell me?"

I stared at his shirt again.

"Willow."

I met his eyes again. "I'm still a virgin."

"Yeah, I figured that out already."

"Well, I...I'm not sure if you'd be okay with not having sex." Good *Lord*, I couldn't believe I was talking to him about this. It had never come up with Brad...I was never comfortable talking to him about it, but with Dash, I already felt like I knew him better than anyone.

"Can't say it'd be easy," he admitted. "But I'm willin' to try if you are."

I rolled my eyes. "You're willing to give up your entire lifestyle in order to 'try'?"

"What kind of lifestyle do you think I have, Willow?"

I blushed, dropping my eyes to the floor again.

"Look at me, baby."

I shook my head and he chuckled. "It's not funny."

He raised an eyebrow. "It kinda is."

I sighed. "I talked to Jasmine last night and she filled me in on a few things."

"Yeah? Like what?"

"Like a biker's tendency to sleep with multiple women…sometimes at the same time. And how there are biker hos who are willing to do anything and everything a biker asks them to do…you know, sexually."

"Do they?"

I smacked his chest. "Now you're teasing me."

He grinned. "Little bit."

I wrinkled my nose. "Is she wrong?"

"No, she's not wrong."

I tried to push away, but he wrapped an arm around me and held firm. "Dash, let me go."

"No. We're gonna hash this out."

"Do we have to hash it out with your arm around me like a vice grip?"

"Yep."

"Alrighty, then," I grumbled.

He grinned. "You like it."

"Maybe."

He dropped his head back and laughed and I couldn't help but smile. "You're gorgeous, you know that?"

"Thank you." I swallowed. "You're extremely pretty yourself."

"Pretty?"

"Definitely."

He chuckled. "Let's make a deal."

"I don't have a costume, nor do I have a lightbulb in

my purse."

He chuckled. "Nice pull."

"Thank you."

"Okay, so this is what we're gonna do." He slid his hands to my neck.

"Lay it on me," I retorted.

"You and I are gonna spend time together. We're gonna get to know each other and see where this leads."

"We are, are we?"

"Yeah." He grinned. "I like you. You like me. It works."

"Until it doesn't," I pointed out. I had next to no experience when it came to relationships (and my one and only experience just went down in flames), so I was nervous that trying to make it work with someone who was the opposite of everything I was used to would fail too.

"Right. But we're gonna make it work until it doesn't."

I studied him for several seconds. "I have no idea how any of this works."

"Neither do I."

I raised an eyebrow. "You have more of an idea than I do."

"How do you figure?"

"I've had one boyfriend. One. He became my fiancé and I just broke up with him," I said. "I'm pretty sure you've got me beat."

"Never had a boyfriend."

I rolled my eyes. "*Dash.*"

He chuckled, leaning down to kiss me again, this time too quickly. "Never had a girlfriend either."

"How does that work, exactly?"

He straightened, taking my hand and leading me back to the sofa where he pulled me onto his lap again. "How it works in my world, is sex without commitment."

"Then how can *this* possibly work? I may not be well-versed in relationships, but I know I can't do casual."

"Don't wanna do casual either," he said.

"So you're okay with not having sex?"

"Not gonna say I'm okay with it, 'cause you're sexy as hell, but I'd never make you do something you didn't wanna do, and I do have some self-control."

I settled my head on his shoulder and sighed. "I could potentially get behind that."

"Yeah?"

"Yes." I sat up. "But will you do something for me?"

"Sure."

"I really want to visit the people in the hospital, and Sam."

Dash sighed. "Tomorrow."

"Why not today?"

"Because you need some time to grieve, Willow."

"I'm going to be grieving for a while, I think, but today I can make sure my friends are okay."

"Tomorrow."

"Are you always this bossy?"

"I protect what's mine, Willow, if that translates into bossy, then, yeah I am." He pulled me closer and I relaxed against him. "Like this, baby."

I closed my eyes and nodded. "I do, too."

My stomach grumbled and Dash chuckled. "Did you eat?"

"No." I sat up again. "I wasn't hungry."

He lifted me off his lap and headed into the kitchen, pulling open the fridge. "Omelet good?"

"You cook?"

"A little, yeah," he said, opening the cabinet that housed the glasses. "Pans?"

"To the right of the stove." I moved to get up, but Dash waved me back down.

"I'm cookin'. You're relaxin'."

"I can at least make another pot of coffee."

He grinned. "That I'll allow."

"Oh, thank you, benevolent one." I chuckled and walked into the pantry to grab the beans. After prepping the coffee, I pressed brew and watched Dash cook. He was actually really impressive for someone who cooks "a little."

"Dash isn't your real name, is it?"

"Nope." He smiled and flipped the omelet. "It's Finn."

"I love that name."

"Yeah?"

I nodded. "It's really cool."

"Thanks. No one calls me that anymore, so I'm not sure I'd even respond."

"So, why Dash?"

"Say, Hi, Finn, out loud, quickly."

"Hi, Finn…oh! Hyphen. Dash." I laughed. "That's a pretty good 'bad' pun."

"You can thank Doc for that."

My arm itched at the memory of the man who stitched me up. "Does he treat people on a regular basis?"

Dash shook his head. "He was a medic in the army and has his medical license, but doesn't go to an office every day. Kind of does his own thing."

I stopped myself from asking more probing questions considering we barely knew each other and it wasn't really any of my business.

"Hey, you okay?" he asked.

I nodded. "I need to take some meds, I think."

"Go get 'em. I'll finish breakfast."

I walked upstairs, gripping the banister as I counted each step, and stalled on the landing. My father's door was slightly open and I could see his neatly made bed through the crack in the door.

For close to an hour I'd been able to forget. Maybe not forget, but pretend it was just a normal working day and he'd walk through the door in time for dinner. I was suddenly hit with the realization that I was truly and tragically an orphan.

Twenty-two years old and totally and completely alone.

"You okay?" Dash called.

I gripped the banister and nodded.

"Willow?"

"Yeah?" I whispered.

Strong arms wrapped around my waist. "What's wrong?"

"Nothing. I'm okay." I turned to face him. "I was just feeling sorry for myself."

"I think you're allowed."

I sighed. "He's never coming back."

"I know."

"What am I going to do when Jazz has to get back to her life? I'll be here all by myself."

"I'll be here anytime you want me."

I smiled. "I appreciate that, but you can't sleep here and I am not a fan of the dark."

"Why can't I sleep here?"

"Because we're not married."

"Right. We'll have to work on changin' your opinion on that."

I rolled my eyes. "Good luck with that. I've had twenty-two years of conditioning."

The doorbell pealed and I sagged against Dash. He kissed my temple. "Go take your meds. I'll grab the door."

I nodded and headed for my room, grateful for the chance to escape.

SEVEN

Dash

I FROWNED AS I walked downstairs and pulled open the front door. I didn't like that Willow was sad…I expected it, sure, but still wasn't happy when it happened.

"Mr. Lloyd?"

"Dash," I corrected.

"Right. I'm Officer Heath. Call me Lisa."

"Yeah, I know who you are," I said somewhat ungraciously, crossing my arms and leaning against the doorframe. "Can I help you with something?"

"I have Willow's phone and purse." She held the items up like they were proof. "I thought we could speak here, rather than have her come down to the station."

"She's not feelin' well," I said. "But I'll give her her personal items. Since you're in the mood for givin' shit back, how about my gun?"

"I really need to get a statement," she replied, ignoring my question

"I really don't give a shit."

She sighed. "Look, I get it, Dash. But I'm not here to jam her up. I like Willow. I just want to help find who did this."

"It sure as fuck wasn't the guys you've got in there now."

"I believe you."

"Yeah? Congratulations. You gonna get them out?"

"I'm working on it."

I glanced at my watch. "It's been two days, work faster."

"Lisa?" I frowned again as Willow gently pushed me aside and smiled at the cop. "Do you have news?"

"No, unfortunately. I brought your phone and purse and wondered if I could take your statement. I thought it would be more comfortable here."

"Oh, yes, right. Um, come on in."

"Willow," I warned. "You *can* say no."

"I know. It's okay," she said. "I trust Lisa."

I grunted, but stepped aside so the cop could walk inside. She handed Willow her personal items and Willow thanked her as she led her further into the house. I bolted the front door, determined not to let anyone else in who didn't have Willow's best interest in mind.

I was about to walk toward the kitchen when the doorbell rang again. I unlocked the door and found some asshole standing on Willow's front porch. "Who the fuck are you?"

"I'm Levi, Parker's brother. Willow asked me to come and see if I could help."

"Right. Come in."

"Are you Dash?"

"Yeah, man. Nice to meet you."

He shook my hand. "You too. Don't know how I can help you, but I'll see what I can do."

"Appreciate it." I nodded and led him down the hall. "Willow's talkin' to a cop right—"

"Which cop?" he asked, suddenly irritated, and passing me in the hallway.

"Lisa," I said as I followed him.

"Hey, Willow," he said, reaching the kitchen before me. "You good?"

I didn't like his protective tone. Exactly what the hell was going on between him and Willow?

"Hi, Levi," Willow said, closing the distance between them and hugging him…a little too long for my liking.

"You doing okay?" Levi asked, holding her close.

"Yeah, she's good," I said.

Willow glanced at me in question and then released Levi. "I'm doing okay, Levi. Thanks."

I moved between them and squeezed her neck gently. "Need anything?"

"I'm good, Dash." She stared up at me, her eyes widening slightly. "Good. Got it?"

I gave her a slight smile. "Got it, Willow."

"Do you, Dash?" she challenged.

"Yeah. Moppin' up what you're spillin'."

"Good for you." She smiled and pulled away from me. "Levi, can I get you anything?"

"Do you have any coffee?"

"Yeah, I can make some."

"I'll take some if you're offering," Lisa said.

"I'll make it, Willow," I said, and headed into the pantry.

"I'll show you where everything is." Willow followed, boxing me in, standing on her tiptoes and giving me a quick kiss. "Thanks," she whispered.

I grinned. "For what?"

"For protecting me...even though it's not really needed." She patted my chest. "I appreciate it."

"You trust these people?"

"Very much so. Lisa's a straight shooter. I know you don't trust the police, but she's never lied to me, and also doesn't like several of the people in power over her."

"Can't imagine when she'd have a reason to lie to you."

"Me neither," she conceded. "But I trust her and I will until she gives me a reason not to. Fair?"

"Yeah, baby, fair."

She smiled. "Okay, here's the coffee, you can figure out the coffee maker, I'm sure."

I leaned down and kissed her one more time. "Like that, Willow."

She smiled, her face pinkening. "Me too."

I let her leave, but took a minute to wipe the goofy grin off my face before grabbing the coffee and busying myself making a pot.

* * *

Willow

I TOOK A couple of quiet breaths as I made my way back to the sofa and sat across from Lisa. I was glad Levi was there, but he was watching me closely and I knew he'd pepper me with questions later. He was almost as protective of me and Jasmine as he was of Parker, so I knew he'd want some answers about Dash and the nature of our relationship.

What it was, anyway.

"Can you walk me through what happened?" Lisa asked.

"I can try."

"Do you mind if I record it?"

"It's fine," Levi said. "But if I don't like the line of questioning, I'm going to stop the interview."

"Are you acting as Willow's attorney, Mr. Powers?" Lisa asked.

"Does she need one?" he challenged.

"No."

"Then, no, I'm not. I'm acting as her friend who happens to be an attorney."

Lisa pulled out her recorder and pressed record. "Walk me through yesterday," she guided. "Start at the beginning."

I closed my eyes and took a deep breath, glancing to my left when I felt the sofa dip. Dash sat beside me and wrapped an arm around my waist, giving me a bolstering smile. I relayed the story and tried my best not to break down. "I met Dad at the church a little after four. I was going to help him run through this Sunday's sermon, and then help clean up after bible study. We had three, maybe four groups meeting that afternoon. I'll get a full schedule from Elean…" I gripped Dash's hand. "Oh, Eleanor, you poor thing." I said, unsuccessfully fighting back tears. "I'm sorry."

"It's okay," Lisa encouraged. "You're doing great. What else do you remember?"

"My father was standing at his desk and I was sitting in the big chair on the opposite side of the room. I was taking notes, offering my opinions, that sort of thing, when I heard two loud gunshots."

"How did you know they were gunshots?" Lisa asked.

For some reason, this question made my arm burn and I laid my hand over the bandage. "I've lived in Georgia all my life, so I've been around hunters' guns all my life. These were unmistakably gunshots, large caliber, and very close. My father must have known as well, because he immediately motioned for me to get in the closet. He was right behind me, and I thought he was going to get in as well, but he told me to be quiet, and before I could protest, shut the door just as his office door was kicked in."

"Did you see who kicked the door down?" Lisa asked.

"No, I could only hear them at this point. My father asked him what he wanted, but the man just yelled at him to shut up and sit down. My father told him there was no money or valuables on church property, and then he shot him...in the knee." Tears flooded my eyes again. "I could hear him drop to the floor...and he was in so much pain. I peeked through the slats in the door."

Dash squeezed my hand and pulled me close. "It's okay, Willow," he said, his voice full of concern. "We can do this another time, can't we?" He looked at Lisa.

"The more information we can gather now, the better," she said. "While the memories are fresh."

I took a deep breath. "It's okay, I want to do this now...I need to."

"What else did the man say?"

"My ears were ringing from the gunshot, but I heard him say something to Dad about Terrance...or...Torrance. It was Torrance, but my father said he didn't want a part in any of it."

"What did he mean by that?"

"I don't know. I'd never heard the name before. I couldn't make out everything they were saying, but I could tell my dad was starting to have trouble breathing. I opened the closet door shutters a little more, just enough to see a tall man, dressed in all black, with a ski mask, standing over him with a gun."

"You're doing great. What happened then?"

"The man told Dad this all would have gone a lot easier for him if he would have just signed. He said property around here was going for an arm and a leg, and then he...laughed and said since he'd already given a leg, why not an arm? Then he...shot him again...in the arm."

"You'd better hope your people find this sick son of a

bitch before I do," Dash said.

"I'm going to pretend like I didn't hear that," Lisa said to him in an icy tone.

"I was so scared, but I could hear Daddy crying out in pain, and just wanted to help him. My hand reached up to the door, just as a second man came in to the room. He asked the first man what the…"F" he was doing and then he shot my dad twice…and Daddy stopped moving. My hand went to my mouth to stop from screaming and that's when I felt and saw that I had been shot. A bullet must have ricocheted and hit my arm."

"How did you end up at the bar?"

"The two men left right after shooting my father, but I was frozen for a few seconds. I was unable to move or make a sound. I heard several more shots in the distance and that's when I opened the door and went to my father. I must have been going into shock because I don't remember entirely what happened after that, just snapshots. I remember running to the bar, and I remember Doc looking at my injuries and I remember Dash's face."

"And you don't have any idea who these men were, or what they wanted from your father?"

"I don't know anything." I bit my lip. "I don't know who or what Torrance is, why these men would kill two women, a child and a small-town church pastor, or how he's wrapped up in any of this. Everything was okay Saturday morning. Why would they do this?"

"That's exactly what I plan to find out, Willow," Lisa said, and shut off the recorder. "Okay, I think this is all I need for now."

"So, we can get Dash's friends out of jail now?" I asked.

"That's not my call."

"Well, I'm coming down to the station to talk to the person whose call it is," Levi said, standing. "They can't hold them any longer without booking them, so they're going to have to shit or get off the pot."

"I think that would be a good idea," Lisa agreed.

"Do you need me to come as well?" I asked.

"No," Levi said. "Dash, if you can give me a list of the guys, I'll see what I can do."

"I'll get you some paper," I offered and headed to the kitchen.

Dash followed and scratched out a few names, handing the list to Levi. Levi slid it into his pocket, set his coffee cup in the sink, and then walked Lisa out. I listened to my voicemail while Dash locked up, then met me in the kitchen again. I was busying myself at the sink, rinsing dishes.

"Why don't you leave those?" he asked.

"Because I can't deal with mess."

He smiled. "OCD. Got it."

"The coroner called," I whispered.

"When?"

"While I was talking to Lisa." I rinsed a mug…again, then set it in the dishwasher. "They're releasing my dad on Tuesday."

"Fuck, baby. You okay?"

I shook my head.

He walked around the island and guided me to his chest.

I held my arms out. "My hands are wet."

"I don't care," he said, pulling me close. "You're gonna tell me what they said while we stand here."

I took a deep breath. "They just said he'll be released on Tuesday and I need to call to let them know where to send him."

"I'll call some of those places, yeah?"

I nodded.

"Did your dad say what he wanted done?"

I nodded again. "He left a living will. After Mama passed, he wanted me to be prepared. But how could I possibly be prepared for this?" I burst into tears and clung to him.

He slid his hand into my hair and stroked my back. He said nothing, just held me and it was everything to me. I wrapped my arms around his waist and gripped him tight.

"I'm sorry," I rasped. "I keep crying all over you."

I tried to pull away, but he held firm. "What did I tell you?"

"I know, but you didn't really sign up for this."

He met my eyes. "I'm not goin' anywhere."

"I'm giving you an out, Dash."

"I don't want an out."

I squeezed my eyes shut. "We can't start a relationship born out of tragedy."

"You don't think?"

"I can't have you bailing in the middle, Dash."

"Do I look like I'm bailin'?"

"If—"

"I'm not goin' anywhere, Willow." He raised my head and wiped my tears away. "Look at me. I want you to see me."

I took a deep breath and stared at him.

"I'm here." He cupped my face. "For as long as you need and want me. I'm not Brad—"

"I know you're not Brad."

He tapped my temple gently. "In here, you know I'm not Brad." He moved his hand to my chest, just above my heart. "But I need you to know here."

I nodded, tears streaming down my face. "I want to."

He smiled. "That's a good first step. Second step is to move forward assuming I'll be there…'cause I will."

"Okay."

"Okay." He kissed me gently. "When you're feeling better, find the will and I'll help you make the arrangements."

I sagged against him. "Thank you."

He gave me a gentle squeeze. "You're welcome."

EIGHT

Willow

Three weeks later...

EVERYTHING WAS OVER. At least the release of the pseudo-innocent and the burying of the people we loved the most. My dad had insisted his body be donated to science, so that was what I did. I'd always been philosophical about death...our bodies were simply the vessel for our real person...our soul, but admittedly, it was strange not having a place to go where he physically was.

Eleanor and Taylor were buried side-by-side, so I found myself visiting their graves several times...and talking to my dad.

Richard Waters had insisted on a memorial service,

and his wife planned the entire event...and what an event it was. It was over the top and gauche, and I knew my dad would have hated it. But I was numb. I didn't care, so I just let them do whatever the heck they wanted. This wasn't about me, after all. I was grieving...in private, but others needed to grieve in public, and I understood that.

Brad had come with his parents and they'd fussed over me in the most skin-crawling way. He'd inserted himself in the family pews and I didn't miss Dash giving me space. The problem was, I didn't want space. I wanted *him*.

The pain in my arm was replaced by an annoying itch. I was grateful that, at the very least, the itch wasn't constant, but it was annoying as heck. I had a really fabulous scar (said no girl ever), and I wasn't particularly happy that I wouldn't be able to wear spaghetti straps...or anything sleeveless until the scar faded.

I'd been informed by my father's lawyer that, not only was the house mortgage-free, he'd left me a life insurance policy worth $900,000. Even my college tuition and books were paid up to date. To say I was surprised was an understatement. We'd never been rich, never had a whole lot of money for extras, but now I could afford to breathe.

Hatch had waited to return home until after the memorial service, Maisie had even flown in for the day before and day after, which I thought was unbelievably kind of them. It was like Hatch knew I needed the kind man who'd showed me his motorcycle so many years ago. He certainly stepped into a fatherly role as I took the time to remember mine. He stayed close (as did Dash) and ushered me away when he could tell I was about to lose it...and yet, no word from Brad. I wouldn't have been able to get through any of this without this "degenerate" biker club, and I was beginning to rethink several things I'd been led to believe.

EIGHT

Willow

Three weeks later...

EVERYTHING WAS OVER. At least the release of the pseudo-innocent and the burying of the people we loved the most. My dad had insisted his body be donated to science, so that was what I did. I'd always been philosophical about death...our bodies were simply the vessel for our real person...our soul, but admittedly, it was strange not having a place to go where he physically was.

Eleanor and Taylor were buried side-by-side, so I found myself visiting their graves several times...and talking to my dad.

Richard Waters had insisted on a memorial service,

and his wife planned the entire event...and what an event it was. It was over the top and gauche, and I knew my dad would have hated it. But I was numb. I didn't care, so I just let them do whatever the heck they wanted. This wasn't about me, after all. I was grieving...in private, but others needed to grieve in public, and I understood that.

Brad had come with his parents and they'd fussed over me in the most skin-crawling way. He'd inserted himself in the family pews and I didn't miss Dash giving me space. The problem was, I didn't want space. I wanted *him*.

The pain in my arm was replaced by an annoying itch. I was grateful that, at the very least, the itch wasn't constant, but it was annoying as heck. I had a really fabulous scar (said no girl ever), and I wasn't particularly happy that I wouldn't be able to wear spaghetti straps...or anything sleeveless until the scar faded.

I'd been informed by my father's lawyer that, not only was the house mortgage-free, he'd left me a life insurance policy worth $900,000. Even my college tuition and books were paid up to date. To say I was surprised was an understatement. We'd never been rich, never had a whole lot of money for extras, but now I could afford to breathe.

Hatch had waited to return home until after the memorial service, Maisie had even flown in for the day before and day after, which I thought was unbelievably kind of them. It was like Hatch knew I needed the kind man who'd showed me his motorcycle so many years ago. He certainly stepped into a fatherly role as I took the time to remember mine. He stayed close (as did Dash) and ushered me away when he could tell I was about to lose it...and yet, no word from Brad. I wouldn't have been able to get through any of this without this "degenerate" biker club, and I was beginning to rethink several things I'd been led to believe.

Dash was still 'here.' He'd made sure I wasn't alone, having gone so far as to form a tight bond with my two best friends. Jasmine and Parker adored him, and even Levi had come to respect him, although, Dash was never okay with him and I being alone. It was almost as though Dash had some kind of scheduling system to ensure someone was always with me when he couldn't.

Tonight was the exception. Dash had something to do with the club and Jasmine, Parker, and Levi had previous engagements, which meant I would need to figure out how to be alone for a few hours. Although I'd insisted all was good in an attempt to force Dash to do what he needed to do, I turned every light on in the house and walked the perimeter checking locks at least three times before I headed to bed.

I'd promised I'd text Dash before I fell asleep, so I did, but now I was awoken by the sound of what I thought might be footsteps.

I listened for a few seconds and all was silent, so I settled back into the pillows.

Creak.

I sat up, grabbed my phone, and for some weird reason, I smoothed my bed. I tended to sleep in one spot all night, so my bed always looked neat, but I wanted it to look as though it wasn't slept in. I moved as quietly as I could to my closet and closed myself in, texting Dash, and then dialing 9-1-1.

"9-1-1, what's your emergency?"

"My name is Willow Miller, I think someone's in my house," I whispered.

"What's your address?"

I whispered the address, then squeezed my eyes shut.

"Stay on the line with me, but you don't have to speak," the kind woman said. "I'm sending an officer to your house."

It felt like I was in the dark forever. My heart raced and my stomach roiled, not knowing what was going on (if anything). I'd never been so scared in my life and all I wanted was for Dash to find me and make me feel safe again.

* * *

Dash

"FUCK!" I HISSED, my heart racing as I read the text from Willow.

"What's up?" Badger asked.

"Someone's in Willow's house. I gotta go, man."

"Go. I got this."

I nodded and headed out the back of the bar, climbing onto my bike and racing to Willow's. I parked just down the street so the pipes wouldn't alert the asshole in the house and then I ran.

I had a key so I let myself in as quietly as I could, not happy that every light in the house was on. Next time I wouldn't listen to her about being 'fine' on her own for a few hours. Fuck!

I walked through the house, discovering the screen to the back window had been cut and the window forced open, but no other indication that someone had been here…and they were gone now. I slid my gun back into my holster and headed upstairs.

"Willow?" I called as I approached her bedroom. "Baby, it's me."

"In here," she rasped.

I pulled open her closet and swore. She'd made herself as small as she could in the corner, wearing nothing but a cami and pair of panties. I squatted down and held my hand out. "You're safe, baby."

She shot out of the closet so fast, I fell on my ass as I

caught her. "Hey, I've got you."

She wrapped her legs around me and I tried not to react. Her pussy was pressed against me with only a thin layer of cotton between us.

"I might be overreacting, but I was so scared," she whispered against my neck, even as she held me tighter.

"You're not overreacting."

She met my eyes. "Someone was really here?"

"Yeah." I stroked her cheek. "Your screen is cut and the window's jacked up in the family room."

She gasped. "Oh, my word."

Sirens were approaching, so I shifted so I could stand up. "You need to put some clothes on, Willow. You can freak out in a minute."

She nodded and pulled on sweats and a hoodie, zipping it to her neck just as cops slammed through the door. Willow jumped, so I pulled her close and kissed her temple. "Willow!"

Willow tried to pull away from me, but I held her tighter as she called out, "Lisa?"

"Yeah, it's me."

"I'll be right there," Willow said, and grabbed my hand. "I'm okay."

I nodded and stepped in front of her to lead her down the stairs. Lisa met us at the bottom. "Whoever was here is gone now," I said.

Lisa nodded. "Yeah. We're collecting evidence now. Have you got somewhere to stay for a few days, Willow?"

"She's coming with me," I said.

"But—"

"Not up for discussion," I ground out.

Willow frowned up at me but didn't contradict me again.

"You good?" I asked Lisa. "Want Willow to pack a bag so we can get the fuck out of here."

"Yeah," she said. "I'll get what we need before you go,

but you can pack, Willow."

Willow said nothing as she stomped up the stairs (her little feet pounding the carpet like she imagined my face on each step). I grinned because she was cute as hell, but schooled my features when she closed us into her room. "I can't stay with you," she snapped, dragging a bag out of her closet.

"Don't have a choice, Willow."

"What will people think?"

"Who gives a fuck?"

"*I* do." She threw the bag on the bed and started throwing clothes into it. "I would *love* to have your devil may care attitude and not care about what people think of me, but I don't." She faced me, an expression of irritation covering her beautiful face.

I closed the distance between us and kissed her gently. I couldn't help myself. She was fuckin' adorable when she was pissed.

"Dash," she hissed.

"My turn to talk," I said, cupping her face.

She huffed, but didn't comment.

"Someone broke into your house and I don't want to think about what they wanted, or what they might have done to you if they'd found you," I said. "There's only one place that's safe for you right now. One place I know no one can get you. And it's *my* place. With me. And my brothers."

"Why is this happening?"

"I don't know, baby, but we're gonna find out. In the meantime, you'll be protected, hear me?" She nodded and I pulled her close. "Pack for at least a week."

"I have school."

"You've got six weeks before school starts," I countered. "This'll be dealt with or you'll be gettin' an escort to your classes."

"Dash."

"Willow," I mimicked.

"Fine," she breathed out.

"Yeah, baby, I know it's fine."

"Well, thank you for making it seem like I had a choice," she snapped.

"You're welcome," I deadpanned.

She pulled away and continued to throw things into her bag and I pulled my phone out of my pocket.

* * *

Willow

I WAS BOTH irritated and relieved as Dash put a call in to Doc and organized someone to watch my house…while I prepared to walk into his den of sin and temptation.

I didn't know how I was going to deal with being alone with Dash in his room at the compound. I was already dealing with impure thoughts when it came to him, and now I was going to be somewhere no one would tell me that ripping his clothes off and licking his entire body would be wrong.

Once I threw the plainest clothes I had into the bag, I made my way to the bathroom for some personal items, before walking back to my room and straight into Dash's arms. He slid his hand to my neck and kissed me deeply, his tongue meeting mine and then diving in deeper. I sighed against his mouth and leaned in, frustrated that I couldn't get closer.

I dropped my shampoo and deodorant on the floor, and wrapped my arms around his waist, sliding my hands up his back. As we grew close to the point of no return, he broke the kiss and dropped his forehead to mine. "Damn."

"This isn't going to work, Dash."

"We'll make it work, baby. You need to be safe."

I sighed, pulling away from him. "My issue is I'm not safe with you either."

"What the fuck?"

"Not like that," I rushed to assure him.

He picked up my discarded items and handed them to me before crossing his arms. "Then like what?"

I didn't know if I could tell him…confess my thoughts. I'd never said anything like that out loud, but he looked both angry and worried, so I knew I needed to tell him why I felt off-kilter.

"Willow?" he prodded.

"You're infuriating sometimes, you know that, right?"

"Backatcha," he ground out. "Now, explain why you don't feel safe."

I focused back on him and swallowed. Then I shook my head.

"Baby," he said, his tone a little gentler.

"Good Lord, Dash, I can't be alone with you or I'll get pregnant."

"Excuse me?"

"All I ever seem to want to do when we're alone is rip your clothes off. If I go to the compound with you, there'll be no one to stop us from…participating in those carnal pleasures," I whispered.

Dash dropped his head back and laughed.

"Very funny." I threw the rest of my things in my bag and tried not to hit him. As soon as my hands were empty, Dash pulled me against his body again.

"I'm not laughing at you, baby."

"Coulda fooled me."

"Okay, maybe your mouth speaking 'carnal pleasures' caught me off-guard, but that's what makes you adorable."

I wrinkled my nose. "I shouldn't be thinking about these things."

"Baby, it's normal to think about 'these things.' It doesn't make you bad."

"You don't know all the things I'm thinking."

Dash raised an eyebrow. "Oh, *really?*"

I smacked his chest gently, my face flaming. "You are ruining me."

"Eyes, baby." He stroked my cheeks and I forced myself to look at him. "Fuck me, you're so beautiful."

"Dash," I whispered.

"No one can ruin you, Willow, unless it's in a good way. You're the kindest person I know and you're good through and through, so I want you to stop beating yourself up about this. We have a connection, a really deep connection, and it's only growin'. Don't dirty that. It's beautiful, like you."

I blinked back tears. "I just don't want to do anything wrong."

"You're not doin' anything wrong, Willow. You're doin' the best you can and doin' it well. I get that you've got some tapes playin' in your head that are just plain wrong, but I'm here to help you sort those out."

I dropped my face to his chest and hugged him tight. "Promise me you won't let me ravish you."

"No."

"Dash."

He chuckled again. "Baby, you wanna rip my clothes off and ravish me, I'm not goin' to stop you, but I will promise that I won't let you do anything before you're ready to do it."

I frowned. "That doesn't make me feel any better."

"Why not?"

"Because I'm pretty sure I'm ready now...at least my body is...and that both scares the crap out of me...and makes me excited."

Dash grinned, kissing me again. "It's okay, Willow. I promise."

I nodded, letting him hold me for a few precious minutes before pulling away. "I'm ready."

He squeezed my hand, grabbed my bag, then led me downstairs.

NINE

Willow

DASH AND I had walked into the compound and I couldn't help but be impressed. It was housed in an old tobacco barn on almost thirty acres, but there were newer, smaller buildings surrounding it. Fencing and concrete walls made the land impenetrable, along with the armed men guarding it.

The main room of the barn was all wood and open, probably like it had been back in the day. There were three sets of stairs, one off the main room, one off the kitchen at the back and one off the foyer.

We took the ones off the main room, and then Dash led me down a hallway on the right and into his room. I was surprised by how modern the room was with a large bed and private bathroom. He also had an a/c unit that was working overtime and I sighed as I walked into the cool space. Summer was hitting Savannah like Satan's cookout, and my home didn't have a/c, so this was a treat for me.

"If it's too cold in here—"

"Don't you dare touch that," I demanded as Dash walked toward the unit. "It feels amazing."

Dash chuckled. "Got it."

"The room is really nice."

He smiled. "Had one of the girls clean it. She did a good job."

I frowned, but kept my opinion to myself. I didn't like that another woman was in his room, even if she was cleaning it. I faced my bag, which Dash had set on the bed.

"Willow?"

"What?"

His arms slid around my waist from behind and he kissed my neck. "You jealous?"

I squeezed my eyes shut. "A little bit, yes."

He turned me to face him and smiled. "Only two people have a key to my room. Me and Doc. I asked Doc to let one of the girls in to clean, but he wouldn't have given her a key. I don't even know who did it."

"It's not that I don't trust you."

"I get it." He kissed me gently. "It'd be a little weird for me too."

I forced a smile. "Sorry."

"Willow," he admonished. "Don't do that. You get to feel however you want to feel."

I nodded, kissing him again. "Okay."

"I have to go."

"What? Why?"

"'Cause I got interrupted and I gotta close the loop on what I was doin'."

"Right. I didn't even think about that." I bit my lip.

"Sorry I pulled you away."

"It's all good. Badger covered it, just gotta make sure."

"Okay."

"Got beers in the fridge, cable on the television, and if you get hungry, there's food in the kitchen downstairs. Just help yourself."

"I don't want to intrude."

"You won't." He patted my hip. "No one'll bug you, Willow, but if you feel uncomfortable for any reason, text me."

I nodded, but truth be told, I probably wouldn't.

"I'll see you when I'm done."

"Okay."

He kissed me, then walked out the door.

I'd hung out in his room, watched a sappy movie, then found myself starving. It was past nine when I ventured my way downstairs looking for coffee. I found it being prepared by a man who looked a bit like my dad…if my dad had longer hair, a scruffy beard, and tattoos.

"Hey, babe," he said. "You Dash's woman?"

I nodded. "My name's Willow."

"Gator."

"Nice to meet you."

"You too. You want coffee?"

I breathed out, "I would *love* some coffee."

He grinned. "That's what I like to hear."

Gator showed me where everything was and then gave me a tour once I had a cup of life in my hands. No one else was around, which seemed odd to me since Dash said the compound was usually milling with people by ten in the morning.

"Why's it so empty?" I asked.

"Late night."

"Oh." I smiled to keep myself from asking anymore questions.

"You hungry?"

"A little, yes."

Gator grinned. "Bacon, eggs, and toast sound good?"

My stomach rumbled. "Oh, my word, yes, please."

He chuckled and led me back to the kitchen, waving to a bar stool by the big stainless-steel island. "Pop yourself there and I'll cook."

"You sure I can't help?"

"Nope. You just sit there and look pretty."

I did as he ordered, my heart warming at the sweet, fatherly way he had about him...despite the fact he looked like a hardcore biker. I was beginning to realize that the things I'd been taught to believe were wrong. Now I just had to figure out how to process that.

I had just buttered two pieces of toast when one was swiped off my plate and lips kissed the back of my neck.

"If this isn't Dash, sir, you'll have a lot of explaining to do," I retorted.

He chuckled and sat beside me. "Hey, baby."

"Hi."

"You hungry?" Gator asked.

"Yeah, man." Dash nodded toward the stove. "You cookin'?"

"Only 'cause I'm fallin' in love with your girl."

I blushed and dropped my eyes to my plate. Dash wrapped an arm around my waist. "She's pretty fuckin' awesome."

"Because I get you free food?" I challenged.

"Well, yeah? Why else?"

I grinned as I leaned into him. "Glad to see your priorities are intact."

He smiled. "You get any sleep?"

"No. I watched a movie and then came down here," I said. "How did your thing go?"

"Good. Wanna crash for a bit though. You good with that?"

I nodded and sat quietly while Dash ate. Since Gator

cooked, I insisted on doing the dishes, then Dash and I headed back to his room. He stepped into the bathroom, walking out with only a pair of boxer briefs on.

"Dash!" I spun and faced the door.

"My shit's in here, baby. It was either walk out in these or naked. I chose the former."

I squeezed my eyes shut wishing he'd chose naked, but said, "Well, thank you for not coming out naked."

I jumped a little when his arms wrapped around me and he kissed my shoulder. "If you'd ever like to walk around in just your panties, I won't complain, FYI."

I sighed. "I have to admit, you look pretty good in just your panties."

Dash laughed. "That sounds all fuckin' kinds of wrong, but you *are* funny."

I smiled, keeping my eyes closed.

"I'm decent, Willow, you can turn around now."

I did so and groaned.

"What?" he asked.

"Why do you have to be so darn perfect looking?"

He had a Dogs of Fire tattoo on his left bicep, a dragon on his right, along with a skull up by his shoulder and an intricate heart on his right forearm. His chest was covered in tattoos and I desperately wanted to trace them all with my tongue.

"Backatcha."

He kissed me, lifting me and settling me on his bed. He slid my sweats off my body, panties and all, settling his face between my legs and kissing me intimately.

"Dash," I rasped, pushing my body back to get some distance. "What are you doing?"

He grabbed my ankles and kept me in place.

"Dash?" I pressed.

"Do you need a play-by-play here, baby?"

"Yes, I think I do," I squeaked.

He grinned. "My plan is to go down on you, and that

means, I'm gonna feast on your pussy."

"No."

"Yes."

"Gross, no."

"Not gross," he argued. "Beautiful. Trust me?"

"In theory, yes."

He tugged me back toward him and leaned over me. "When my tongue hits your clit, you'll understand what I'm talking about, and you'll love it. I promise."

I felt the heat creep up my face. "I can't believe you just said that."

"I plan to lick every inch of your pussy, too, baby, so get ready."

I groaned covering my face with my hands.

"Eyes, Willow."

I shook my head.

"Willow," he warned, kissing my knee.

"I can't look right now," I mumbled. "Please don't stop, but don't make me watch."

"Baby."

"*Please,* Dash. I trust you, but I need to not look right now."

His mouth traveled down my leg again, then covered my very private part. I writhed as he gently sucked on my clitoris and I couldn't stop myself from bucking against his mouth. This made him grip my thighs harder and keep me in place, but it did not make him remove his mouth. I let out a quiet squeak as his tongue, then his finger, slipped inside of me and I was overwhelmed with the sensation. His mouth moved back to my clit and he slipped another finger inside of me and I whimpered as I came apart.

I gathered my courage and glanced down my body to watch as he continued to kiss me intimately and then he raised up and leaned over me. "You taste like honey, baby."

"I...I don't really have words."

Dash grinned as he kissed his way to my neck, cupping my breast as he kissed me just under my jaw. "You don't need to say anything."

Despite the overwhelming ecstasy he was creating, guilt won out and I asked him to stop.

"Baby."

I dragged my hands down my face and groaned. "I'm sorry. I just...can't."

He pulled me onto his chest. "It's okay."

I squeezed my eyes shut. "I loved everything you did, but I feel so unbelievably dirty."

"Nothin' we did here was dirty, Willow, but I get it."

I swallowed. "You don't have to lie."

"Exactly which part am I'm fuckin' lyin' about?"

"The getting it part."

"I *do* get it," he said. "Don't mean I like it, but I'm not gonna make you do anything you don't feel comfortable with, and I'm not gonna be a dick while you're figurin' it out."

I snuggled closer to him. "I appreciate that."

"Let's get some sleep."

I nodded. Dash stepped into the bathroom and was there a while...I didn't ask why, but I threw on some clothes while he was in there and climbed under the covers. Dash joined me (finally) and then he wrapped his arms around me and we slept.

* * *

THE NEXT MORNING, I had just pulled my hair up into a scrunchy when my phone pealed. I grabbed it and saw it was Lisa calling. "Hi, Lisa."

"Hey, Willow. I just wanted to let you know, we've got everything we need from your house and you're free to go back."

"Okay, thanks. Did you find anything?"

"Got a nice palm print on the window casing, but no hits on A.F.I.S. yet."

I nodded. "Okay. Thanks."

"Just be careful, okay? I can have a car on your place for a while, but probably a good idea not to stay there alone until this is sorted."

I glanced at Dash and said, "I'll talk to Dash and let you know what the plan is."

"Sounds good. Text me when you plan to head back to your house, I'll get a car on you."

"Okay, thanks Lisa."

"Talk to you soon."

She hung up and I dropped my phone on the side table again and filled Dash in on the conversation.

"You can stay here for a while, Willow," he said. "Or I can stay at your place…or we can do both."

"I'll call Jazz."

Dash closed the distance between us and shook his head. "You're not understandin'. You and I are together going forward. You're never without me or one of my brothers. I can stay with you full-time, except for the times when you're here, but it's you and me, Willow. Not Jazz."

"You're suggesting we move in together?"

"Temporarily…yeah."

I shook my head. "We can't live together, Dash."

"Goddammit, Willow, this is serious. Wrap your fuckin' mind around the fact that you and I are joined at the hip until all of this is done, or you're gonna be miserable for a while."

"Don't talk to me like that," I snapped.

"I'm trying to make you understand how serious this is!"

"And you're assuming I don't understand?" I threw my hands in the air. "Thank you for being a jerk." I stormed out of his room and downstairs, heading out the back door and jogging toward…I had no idea. I just ran.

I found myself at the edge of the property with nowhere to go except through the trees or back the way I came...and I didn't want to do either. So, I flopped onto my butt and dropped my head to my updrawn knees.

A few minutes later, I heard footsteps behind me, but didn't look up. I knew who it was and I wasn't really interested in having another fight.

"Heard you're havin' a rough day."

"Hi, Gator." I glanced to my right. "I thought you were Dash."

"Nope, you got me," he said, sitting beside me and wrapping his arms around his knees. "Don't know that that'll be for very long, 'cause he's worried about you, but I asked if I could talk to you a bit."

"Why?"

"Because you lost your daddy and I lost my little girl. I figure you and I have a few things in common."

"You lost your little girl?"

"Yeah. It was a long time ago, but I think about her every day."

I stared out at the trees. "I'm sorry, Gator."

"Thanks."

"I don't really know how to do anything without him. He tried to raise me to be independent, but I'm not very good at it."

"You'll figure it out. You would have even if he was still here, now you just have to do it a little sooner." He patted my arm. "But you're not alone."

I gave him a sad smile. "I know, but sometimes it doesn't feel that way."

"Oh, I hear that." He wrapped an arm around my shoulders. "But that feeling goes away."

I blinked back tears. "I wish I could believe you."

"I know. You will eventually."

"I got this, Gator," Dash said, and plopped down on my other side.

I smiled at the older man. "Thanks, Gator."

"You need me, you let me know."

"I will," I promised.

Gator left us and Dash pulled me into his arms. "I'm sorry, baby."

"So am I."

"Sometimes I forget to be patient."

I smiled. "So do I."

"Whatever you need, I've got you…unless it puts you in danger."

"Okay." I sighed. "I will try and get used to all of this, it's just so out of my realm of experience."

"I know." He kissed my temple.

"I'm fine with staying at my house. I need to start figuring out what I'm going to do with it anyway. It's a lot of house for one person and it might be time to sell it."

"You don't have to make any decisions right now, right?"

I shook my head. "No. It can wait."

"So, let's not make any massive decisions while we're still in mourning."

"And let's not talk to me as though I am a child, hmm?"

He grinned. "I can do that."

"How busy are you tomorrow?"

"Why?"

"I think I need to start going through my dad's office, but I don't want to do it alone."

"I can make that happen, Willow."

"Thanks."

"You're welcome." He kissed my temple. "Don't think about it now, though, yeah? We'll deal with everything tomorrow."

"Okay," I said, then groaned. "My butt's wet."

"That's because you're sittin' on wet grass."

"Really, Einstein? Thanks for the clarification."

He chuckled and stood, pulling me up and kissing me quickly. "I've got you, you know that, right?"

"I do know that. I just forget sometimes."

"That's why I'm here to remind you."

"I like that you're here and I like that you're not going anywhere."

"My woman finally gets it," he retorted.

"And I *really* like being your woman."

"Yeah, well, I'm pretty fuckin' fabulous, so you should."

I grinned, kissing him gently. "I think you need to work on that low self-esteem."

"I'll make that a priority."

I laughed and we headed back to the clubhouse.

I smiled at the older man. "Thanks, Gator."

"You need me, you let me know."

"I will," I promised.

Gator left us and Dash pulled me into his arms. "I'm sorry, baby."

"So am I."

"Sometimes I forget to be patient."

I smiled. "So do I."

"Whatever you need, I've got you…unless it puts you in danger."

"Okay." I sighed. "I will try and get used to all of this, it's just so out of my realm of experience."

"I know." He kissed my temple.

"I'm fine with staying at my house. I need to start figuring out what I'm going to do with it anyway. It's a lot of house for one person and it might be time to sell it."

"You don't have to make any decisions right now, right?"

I shook my head. "No. It can wait."

"So, let's not make any massive decisions while we're still in mourning."

"And let's not talk to me as though I am a child, hmm?"

He grinned. "I can do that."

"How busy are you tomorrow?"

"Why?"

"I think I need to start going through my dad's office, but I don't want to do it alone."

"I can make that happen, Willow."

"Thanks."

"You're welcome." He kissed my temple. "Don't think about it now, though, yeah? We'll deal with everything tomorrow."

"Okay," I said, then groaned. "My butt's wet."

"That's because you're sittin' on wet grass."

"Really, Einstein? Thanks for the clarification."

He chuckled and stood, pulling me up and kissing me quickly. "I've got you, you know that, right?"

"I do know that. I just forget sometimes."

"That's why I'm here to remind you."

"I like that you're here and I like that you're not going anywhere."

"My woman finally gets it," he retorted.

"And I *really* like being your woman."

"Yeah, well, I'm pretty fuckin' fabulous, so you should."

I grinned, kissing him gently. "I think you need to work on that low self-esteem."

"I'll make that a priority."

I laughed and we headed back to the clubhouse.

TEN

Willow

AFTER GRABBING MY bag from his room, Dash took me home, but walked into the house before me and did a "sweep." Once he deemed no one was hiding in the corners or the closets, he let me in. Lisa had done as she promised and put a car outside, so I stood on the porch until I was given the all-clear.

Not long after I'd set my bags down in the foyer, a few of Dash's biker brothers arrived to take measurements on the broken screen and window, and install a pretty elaborate security system with cameras and sensors on every door and window.

A month ago, I would have scoffed at the idea of a security system...but a lot had changed in less than four weeks.

As at least six guys milled around my house, I walked into my dad's office and stood at the threshold for a few minutes. I didn't really know where to start. I rarely came in here, mostly because I wasn't particularly interested in his theological study notes and financial documents, but now I had to make some sense of my dad's system and I was at a bit of a loss.

Dash wrapped his arms around me from behind and kissed the back of my neck. "Need help?"

I leaned back against him. "Probably. I just have no idea where to start."

"How about you start on his desk, and I'll have a look at his computer."

I nodded. "Sounds good."

For the next three hours, we waded through paperwork, sermon notes, bank statements, and mostly stacks of trash.

"It's official," I declared, dropping a stack of junk into the recycle pile. "My dad was a packrat."

"You might be right." Dash sat at the shredder, shredding yet another phone bill dad had kept ...he'd been sitting there for an hour.

I scanned the space and sighed. "We've made a bit of a dent at least."

"Yeah," Dash said, feeding more paper into the machine. "I'm getting hungry, you got anything to eat?"

"I don't know what I have, honestly." I dusted off my jeans and settled my hands on my hips. "How about we go shopping first and grab fast food on the way back?"

Dash grinned. "Whatever gets me fed fastest works for me."

"Yeah, I'm pretty hungry myself. I'll go wash up and meet you in the kitchen. We can make a list and go from there."

"Sounds good."

I leaned down and cupped his face. "Thanks for your help."

"You're welcome." He grinned. "Now, kiss your man."

I did and then headed to my room.

I walked into the kitchen to find Dash on his phone, so I grabbed a piece of paper and a pen and started the shopping list. We needed everything...except beer. Dash made sure we were stocked for days with his favorite.

"Yeah, man, that'd be good," Dash said. "Alamo or Gator's good." He glanced at me and then at his watch. "Ten. Yeah, that'll work. Okay, man, thanks."

He hung up and added beer to my list, then pulled open the fridge.

"You gonna fill me in?" I asked.

"Badger, Doc, and I have some shit to do tonight, so Gator or Alamo are gonna come hang with you. They can grab whatever groceries you need."

"Um...why?"

He raised an eyebrow. "Really?"

"Yes, really. They don't need to come...I can call Jazz or Parker."

He grabbed a bottled water and closed the fridge. "No way in hell are you stayin' here without a male presence, Willow."

"I'll call Levi, then."

"No."

"What? Why not?" I demanded. "I've known Levi my whole life."

"Because he wants into your panties, baby, and I'm not comfortable with that."

I snorted. "He does *not* want into my panties. Don't be ridiculous."

Dash moved behind me, sliding his hand between my legs and cupping my mound as he kissed the nape of my neck. "He wants this, Willow. Guaranteed. But it's mine, and until I know I can trust him with you, it's not gonna happen."

His palm pressed against my clitoris and I groaned as I leaned into his touch. "You're ridiculous."

"Maybe so, but I'm not wrong."

He removed his hand and I whimpered. He was the master at wearing my defenses down, but I knew if I let him go on, it wouldn't be fair because I'd eventually shut it down.

"You want more, Willow?" he challenged.

"Yes, but I'm not going to do that to you," I said. "I'd rather talk about where you're going, why, and how long you'll be gone?"

"We can talk about one of those subjects."

I crossed my arms. "What do you mean, *one* of those subjects?"

"Won't discuss Club business, but I should be back in a few hours." He washed his hands, then kissed my cheek. "You want Alamo or Gator to come hang out?"

"I don't know Alamo," I said.

"Then I'll make sure Gator does it." He raised an eyebrow. "You said you agreed, Willow. You gonna give me grief?"

I sighed. "No. Gator's fine. I just wish you'd tell me what you're doing."

"Can't. Not gonna have that conversation again. Club business is off-limits."

"*Club business is off-limits,*" I mimicked in a snotty voice, and stormed out of the room.

I didn't get far.

Dash caught me around the waist and hauled me against his body. "This is the definition of giving me grief, Willow."

"Well, excuse me if I'm asking too many questions, Mr. Lloyd," I ground out. "Sue me."

He chuckled and gave me a gentle squeeze. "Like you

sassy, baby."

"Don't act all sexy right now, Dash, I'm irked."

"I can tell." He kissed the nape of my neck. "But I like that you think I'm sexy even though you're irked."

I shivered. I loved it when he kissed me in the sensitive spot behind my ear. "You're such a butt."

He laughed. "Oh, your clean little mouth just sends me to places in my mind that are not so clean."

I twirled to face him and gripped his shirt. "Are you doing something dangerous?"

"No."

"Then why are you doing it at ten o'clock at night?"

"'Cause we need to get on it right away."

I frowned. "But it's not dangerous?"

He grinned. "No, baby, we'll be at the compound."

"Why can't you meet here?" I asked. He cocked his head and I groaned. "Club business, right?"

"You're gettin' it."

"Well, you just told me two out of the three," I retorted.

He grinned. "Looks like it."

"Are you planning on leaving the compound for any reason?"

He kissed me, but didn't answer my question.

"*Dash.*"

"Baby, we're not having this conversation.

I huffed. "Will you text me if you leave the compound?"

"No, but I'll text Gator."

"And he'll tell me where you're going?"

"Probably not."

I gripped his shirt harder. "I don't like this."

"Baby, it's all good. Nothing's going to happen."

I bit my lip. "Daddy didn't think so either."

"Hey," he said, sliding his hand to my neck. "I'm not doin' anything dangerous, yeah? Badger, Doc, and I have some business to do, but there's no reason for me to leave the compound. I'm protected...so are you."

I wrapped my arms around his waist. "Please don't get yourself shot."

"I won't get myself shot."

I dropped my head to his chest. "Text me every thirty minutes."

"Not gonna do that, baby, but if you're really worried, text me and I'll text you back."

"I think I'm addicted to you now."

He chuckled. "I'm okay with that."

"It's silly, really."

"No, it's not." He hugged me tighter. "We're in the honeymoon phase."

"I guess that's true." I slid my hands up his chest. "I really need you to promise not to get shot."

"Willow," he said, laughing, lifting my face to meet my eyes. "Baby, I'm not gonna get shot."

I wrinkled my nose. "Well, you better not, or I'll hurt you."

"Consider me warned." He leaned down and kissed me and we headed out to take care of our errands.

* * *

Dash

I WALKED INTO the compound still chucklin' at the way Willow kept bargaining to keep me with her. Fuck me, my girl was gorgeous. I wish I coulda done what I had to do at her place, but she couldn't be part of any of it. Plus, I knew I'd need help, maybe even more than my crew could provide.

I headed to the conference room in the back where Badger and Doc were waiting and dropped a folder full of papers and a flash drive I'd stolen from Alfred's office on the table.

"This is what Willow's dad died over."

"What the fuck is this?" Doc asked.

"I'm not exactly sure, but a lot of it has to do with something called the Torrance Group."

"What the hell is the Torrance Group and why would they kill an old preacher, and all those other people?"

"That's exactly what we have to find out." I spread the papers out and handed Badger the flash drive. "And I think we'll find the answers in here. We need to figure out who these Torrance assholes are, and who the fuck's in charge."

Badger plugged the drive into the laptop and we got down to the business of figuring out who was threatening Willow.

"Badger, if you need any help with the tech, call Booker in Portland. Doc'll hook you up if you have any trouble."

"Got it," Badger said. "Right now, all I need is a six pack of blue raspberry Mountain Dew."

"How can you poison yourself with that shit man?" I asked.

"Hey, it's got electrolytes."

Doc laughed. "For a smart guy, you're a fuckin' idiot Badger."

After several hours, we were able to piece together a pretty good picture of who the Torrance Group was. Using what was obviously intel that Alfred had been gathering, we could see the group was a real estate holding company, owned by what appeared to be local investors. We couldn't find any information on who these people were, so either the old man didn't know, there were more files somewhere else, or they were taken from him when he was killed.

"Hey Dash, check this out man!" Badger called out.

"What is it? What am I looking at?"

On his screen was a close-up picture of a clown's face. He had blood dripping from the corners of his mouth and sharp, yellow teeth. His eyes blazed red and his lips were curled in a terrifying sneer.

I scowled. "What the fuck, man?"

"Right? Kind of a strange picture to be on a pastor's computer, isn't it?" he said. "I mean, you'd expect porn or something, but this is messed up shit."

"Shut up, Badger," I snapped. "This is Willow's dad you're talking about."

"Sorry." He shrugged. "Well anyway, I found this picture in a folder labeled TG. I thought it was weird and so I took a closer look at it."

"Weird, how? I mean aside from the obvious," I asked.

"First of all, the image was password protected."

"Why is that strange?"

"Let me put it to you this way. Old peoples' computers are by far the easiest to hack, because they rarely password protect anything, and if they do, they use very simple passwords for everything. For instance, Alfred's windows login is Willow and his email password is Jesus," he said. "How long do you think it took me to figure those out?"

"Thank you, Professor Warren," I retorted. "Now, what does this all have to do with a homicidal demon clown picture?"

"First of all, I thought it was odd that it was the only file on his PC that's protected, and secondly, it didn't use a password that seemed like something the good pastor would have come up with."

"Then how did you get in? Did you call Booker?"

"Look, Dash, I have skills too, ya know. I don't *need*

Booker."

"You totally called Booker, huh?" I challenged.

"I called Booker. But check this out," he said excitedly, switching gears. "Once Booker got me in, I noticed something odd about the file's properties."

"What about them?"

"Here, take a look at the file size. This is just a standard jpeg image file. It should only be around a couple megs right?"

"Sure okay."

"So why is this one 750 gigs?" Before I could retort, he said, "I'll tell you why, because there's information encoded within the image file."

"Badger, remember that thing I said about you being a fuckin' idiot?" I asked.

"I sure do."

"I take it back…you're only half an idiot."

Badger grinned and threw an empty Mountain Dew can at me.

ELEVEN

Willow

TWO A.M. ROLLED around and I was exhausted, but wired. Dash still wasn't back, and even though he'd responded to every text I sent, the responses were short and I just wanted to put my arms around him and make sure he was okay.

"Baby girl, go to bed," Gator ordered.

The man was currently reclined on my sofa, his third beer in his hand, and he was watching some MMA fight while I paced the floor. I wasn't exactly sure what MMA stood for, but I had to assume one of the Ms was for Macho.

"No. I couldn't sleep right now, even if I tried. Plus, now I'm kind of interested to see if the fighting man in the blue chokes the other guy with his ponytail."

Gator laughed, beer spitting out of his mouth, but then he froze.

I heard movement from the front of the house and Gator was off the couch and pushing me toward the powder room faster than I could turn my head.

"Stay there," he ordered, sliding his gun out of his holster.

I stood in the bathroom as quiet as I could until I saw Dash in the doorway. Then it was full steam ahead and I was in his arms, wrapping my legs around his waist so he couldn't get away from me again. "You're back," I breathed out, looping my arms around his neck.

He chuckled, holding me steady. "You gonna greet me like this every time I come home?"

"Maybe."

"I'll need to leave and come back more often then."

"You better not." I met his eyes. "Did you get everything done?"

"Nope, but we were at a good stopping place, so thought I'd come back and get you naked."

I blushed. "Dash."

"What? Gator won't be shocked."

I wrinkled my nose and climbed off him. "But I am."

He grinned, leaning down to kiss me quickly. "Come on. Gator's leaving."

I followed him to the foyer and hugged Gator. "Thanks for watching out for me."

"Anytime, sweetness." He kissed my cheek. "You need me, I'm there."

He left, Dash locked up and set the alarm, and then we headed to my bedroom. We made out a little, but this time he stopped the frustration and insisted we try to sleep. I nodded and he kissed my temple...and I kicked my blankets off, trying to escape the heat.

This one action started a domino effect that ended with

both of us off the bed and readjusting the sheets.

"Just wanted to sleep," Dash grumbled. "But, no. My woman decides she's developed restless leg syndrome."

I rolled my eyes. "I'm sensitive to the heat."

"I think you're sensitive to all the hotness lying next to you."

"Yes, I'm sure that's probably it," I deadpanned. "But just in case it's not, explain to me why it has to be surface of the sun hot?"

"We could always sleep at the compound for a few nights."

"Or I could move."

Dash studied me. "You wanna move?"

I sighed. "Not really, but what am I going to do with a house full of ghosts?"

"Let's get all your dad's stuff dealt with, then make a few decisions…it's almost four in the morning, and now is probably a bad time to be thinking about what to do."

"Probably."

"Come on, baby, let's get some sleep. We have more shit to go through tomorrow."

"Fine," I breathed out dramatically. "But all that movement's made me even hotter."

"You should sleep on top of the covers, then."

"Good idea."

I waited for him to climb in, then I flopped on the bed and got as close to him as the covers would allow.

It wasn't ideal, and I knew I'd need to figure out something else since the ceiling fan just wasn't doing it for me anymore.

* * *

ONE WEEK LATER, we were back in the compound and getting ready for bed. The temperature had skyrocketed over a hundred, and I just couldn't deal anymore, so we were going to hide here until things cooled off a bit. It worked out well, since there was a club get-together the next day, so we planned to sleep in.

He removed his shirt and I reached out and touched his stomach, his abs contracting as I did. "This is just too much."

"Yeah?"

"Oh, my word, '*yeah.*'"

Dash lifted me off my feet and dropped me gently onto the bed as he stretched out beside me and kissed me. His hand slid under my T-shirt and cupped my breast over my bra. I whimpered as he pulled the cup down and rolled my nipple between his fingers.

"Oh!" I squeaked.

His mouth went to my neck. "You okay?"

I arched into his touch. "Yes."

"Want me to keep goin'?"

"Yes," I panted out.

He pushed my shirt off and threw it in the corner, then unclasped my bra and slid it down my arms. I immediately covered myself with my hands. I'd never been this naked in front of anyone and as much as I was enjoying this, it was alien to me.

"Trust me?" he asked, tugging my arms away from my breasts.

I closed my eyes and nodded.

"Look at me, baby."

"I can't," I rasped.

"You keep your eyes closed, Willow, and I'm gonna stop."

It took me a second to find my courage, but I opened them and Dash kissed me quickly. "We stop whenever you want to, yeah?"

I nodded.

"You just say the word."

"Okay."

"You need to keep your eyes open, though. I want to

know what you're thinking."

"You know what I'm thinking when my eyes are open?" I challenged.

"Most of the time," he said.

"I don't know how I feel about that."

"All your secrets are safe with me," he promised, cupping my breast and gently squeezing it. Leaning down, he drew a nipple into his mouth, and then the other. I sighed as he kissed between my breasts and then focused on my mouth again.

He shifted so he was hovering over me, between my legs and I ran my hand down his bare chest, tracing one of his tattoos with my finger.

He kissed me again as he tugged down my sweats, dropping them on the ground. His hand slid under the waistband of my panties and between my legs. I squirmed at his touch, his hand cupping me. "Open, baby."

I shifted so he could slide his hand further between my legs and then he slipped a finger inside of me and I whimpered.

He pulled back. "Does that hurt?"

"Not at all." I grabbed his arm. "Don't stop."

Dash grinned and slid off the bed.

"Where are you going?" I demanded.

"Nowhere, baby," he promised patting my bottom. "Lift."

I lifted my hips and he pulled my panties off and then kissed his way up my legs. Gripping my thighs gently, he settled his face between them and kissed the top of each. "Gorgeous."

"I want to see you," I whispered, and reached up to stroke his cheek. "All of you."

"You sure?"

I nodded. We'd been dancing around this for weeks and I was done listening to the guilt. I was in love with him, and I wanted more.

He smiled and stood, pushing his boxer briefs off.

I swallowed. "Oh, my word."

His expression became one of concern. "What?"

"You're...um...really big."

Dash chuckled and crawled over me, kissing between my breasts. "Trust me?"

I cupped his face as he hovered over me. "Yes."

"I'm gonna take care of you, baby, but you ever want to stop, tell me."

"What if—"

"Doesn't matter what reason, Willow. You want to stop, we stop." I nodded and he leaned closer. "Doesn't matter when or why, yeah?" I nodded again. "I need to hear the words, baby."

"If I want to stop, we stop."

"Exactly," he whispered, and kissed me. He rolled us onto our sides and cupped my bottom, guiding my thigh over his hip. It brought me closer to his body and his cock rubbed against my clit giving me the most incredible sensation. He slid his hand between us and slipped a finger inside. "Soaked, baby."

I nodded. "Is that bad?"

"Not at all. It's perfect." He grinned. "Better than perfect."

"Are you sure?"

"Baby, do you like what I'm doin'?"

I let out a quick breath. "Yes," I panted as he slipped another finger inside of me.

"Then it's perfect."

Before I could say anymore, he kissed me, sliding his tongue into my mouth as I sighed. I heard the tear of foil and then he rolled on a condom and positioned me so I was straddling him, but we were on our sides.

"We're gonna go slow. It'll take your body a little bit to get used to this, but you can pull back if it's too much. It's why we're like this. You have more control."

I nodded. "Okay."

"Are you scared?"

"A little."

"Do you want to stop?"

"Not even a little bit." I bit my lip. "Can I tell you something because I really don't want to be a slut."

"What the fuck? You. Are. Not. A. Slut," he ground out.

"Let me do this." I squeezed my eyes shut again. "I love you. You don't have to say it back, but this wouldn't be happening if it wasn't true and I just wanted you to know that." I met his eyes again. "I think I fell in love with you the second you stood up to Brad, maybe before, but even if it's dumb, it's true. I love you."

He stroked my cheek. "Love you too, Willow."

"You don't have to—"

"Not sayin' it because I feel obligated to. I knew you were special when I saw you in your sundress and boots, but when you stood in the police station wearin' my patch, I knew I was a goner."

I smiled. "I thought you were mad at me."

"No. I was pissed Hatch dragged you to the station, but I also realized my jacket was right where it was supposed to be and that rocked me a little."

I ran my thumb over his mouth. "I like that."

"Me too."

He tilted his hips forward, his cock slipping partially inside of me. "Okay?"

"Yes," I breathed out. "More."

Rolling my nipple between his fingers, I arched, naturally drawing him further into my body. It felt incredible. "Oh!" His head dipped to cover that same nipple with his mouth and he bit down gently as he thrust deeper. "Yes!" I cried.

"Okay?"

"Yes, more."

I shifted and he slid a little deeper, then a little more. All the while, he worked my nipples, my clit, my mouth. I had to give it to him, he waited until I was no longer fully coherent before he gave one swift push and I felt the sting of my virginity leaving my body. He caught my cry with his mouth and stilled, but held me close.

Dash kissed my cheek and whispered, "It's done. Are you okay?"

I smiled, shifting so I could stroke his cheek. "I'm sore, but I don't want to stop yet, okay?"

"You sure?"

I shifted so I could draw him deeper. "Yes, I'm sure."

"You sure you don't want to stop?"

"I need you to stop talking now," I said. "I want more of what we just did."

Dash kissed me and then drew my nipple into his mouth again, then the other. Sliding his hand between us, he fingered my clit and I couldn't help but rock my hips against him, which pulled him further inside of me.

"Yes," I whispered. "Harder."

He thrust into me and I raised my legs, wrapping my ankles around his hips. He continued to surge into me, until my climax overtook me. I screamed his name as I came undone, then he gave one final thrust and grunted, "Mine," and rolled us onto our sides again.

"Yours," I agreed.

"Brace Willow, I'm gonna slide out and it may sting a bit."

"'K." I gripped his shoulders as he moved his hips away from me. He was right, I was a little sore, but it didn't take away from the fact that he'd made my first time incredibly sweet. I hadn't expected I'd hate it, but I certainly didn't expect to enjoy it as much as I did, especially before marriage.

"Don't move," he said, and kissed me gently. "I'll be right back."

I nodded with a smile and he climbed off the bed and headed into the bathroom. I bit my lip in an effort not to squeak at the sight of him walking away. Goodness, he was pretty. I heard the toilet flush and then Dash returned to me with a warm washcloth.

"Spread, baby." I did and he settled the soft cloth against me, soothing the sting. "Feel good?"

"Very," I whispered on a yawn.

He smiled and leaned down to kiss me. "I'm gonna get you a shirt, then we'll sleep."

"Give me a second," I said, and headed to the bathroom. Admittedly, I moved a little slower than normal. I cleaned up a little more and then walked back out to the bedroom and grabbed my panties, shimmying them back on.

Dash wrapped his arms around me, pulling me against his hard, naked chest. He'd pulled on his boxer briefs again, which showed every ridge. "How sore are you?"

I stroked the corded muscle on his neck. "A bit."

"I grabbed a couple of Tylenol for you." He ran his hands over my bottom. "And a T-shirt."

"Thanks."

"Let's get some sleep," Dash said, and pulled the covers down. I slid in and he pulled me against him. I was on my back, my side against him and he settled his head in his palm, hovering above me slightly. "You understand what I meant when I said 'mine'?"

"This is going to happen again?"

Dash. "A lot."

I giggled. "Promises, promises."

"But more than this happenin' a lot, you're mine, Willow. You need to make it permanent, we'll make it permanent."

"It's only been a month or so."

"So?"

"I know how I feel, but I'd still like to get to know you

better…figure out how to live in your world."

"Fair enough."

"I do love you, honey."

"Love how you call me honey, Willow."

"You do?"

He kissed me gently. "Yeah."

I smiled, biting back another yawn.

Dash pulled the covers over us and kissed the top of my head. "Sleep, baby."

"I don't know if I can."

He pulled me close and shut off the light. "Try."

TWELVE

Dash

I WOKE TO an empty bed, and then heard crying coming from my bathroom. I jumped off the mattress and rushed inside to find Willow sitting on the toilet, her head in her hands.

I kneeled in front of her and lifted her head. "What's wrong, baby?"

"I'm going to hell."

I forced myself not to give any indication that I found this slightly funny. "You're not goin' to hell."

"I can't get the blood out of my underwear."

"We'll throw them away, baby, it's no big deal."

She shook her head. "We need to burn them or someone might think someone was murdered."

I couldn't stop a chuckle at this. "Baby, it can't possibly be that bad."

"Oh, it's bad."

"Okay, we'll burn them. We have a couple burn barrels out back."

She gasped. "No one can *see* us, Dash!"

I sat up, wrapping my arms around her and sliding my hands into her hair. "No one will see anything, baby. You're safe here. I won't tell anyone your secrets."

"I can't believe I'm hugging you while I'm on the toilet," she said. "I'm pretty sure this would have never happened with Brad."

"You seriously thinkin' about Brad right now?"

"Only in so much to say that he's a big fat jerk and I love you, but realize now I never really loved him."

"No?"

"No…mostly because there'd be no way I'd hug him on a toilet."

"Fuck me, you're gorgeous."

"I'm glad you think that, this not being my finest hour and all."

I smiled and met her eyes. "You still bleeding?"

She shook her head. "I don't think so."

"You wanna take a shower with me and work out some of that Protestant guilt?"

"Will that work?"

"I don't know. Let's figure it out together."

She sighed and nodded, and I started the shower.

* * *

Willow

DASH PULLED MY T-shirt over my head and gently kissed me before holding my hand while I stepped into the shower. He joined me, guiding me under the spray and gently washing my hair with all the care one would have with a child.

After he rinsed my hair, he kissed me, pressing me against the wall and lifting me so I could wrap my legs around him. Holding me, he managed to grab a condom and put it on before slipping into me and I sighed as his girth filled me.

"Dash," I whispered. My connection to him seemed to ease all of my worries.

"Love you, Willow."

"Love you too, honey."

"Wanna marry you."

"Not really fair to be saying that right now, Dash."

I couldn't believe he said this while he was buried inside of me.

His hand slid to my breast and he rolled my nipple between his fingers. "Don't care, baby."

I smiled. "I can tell."

"I'll ask you the right way, but just givin' you notice, it's gonna happen."

I squeezed him tighter with my legs, drawing him deeper inside of me. "Okay."

He made love to me with a surprising gentleness, considering we were in a shower and there wasn't a whole lot of room. As we cleaned up and then toweled off, I was feeling a whole lot better.

"You good?" he asked, pulling on jeans.

"Really good." I sighed. "Thanks for letting me freak out."

"You can freak out anytime, Willow." He kissed me gently. "Especially considerin' you're fuckin' cute when you're havin' a total breakdown."

I dragged my clothes on and brushed out my hair. "Super glad I could entertain you."

He grinned, kissing me again. "Come on. Let's go find some breakfast."

I nodded and followed him downstairs.

* * *

A FEW HOURS later, the pig was on the spit and people were starting to arrive. The club get-together tonight included friends and family, so Jasmine, Parker, and Levi had all been invited. I was both excited and a little nervous to see how my two worlds would collide…but mostly excited.

I helped a few of the club women with food while Dash went to do whatever badass bikers did. Jasmine and Parker arrived an hour into the party and they both looked adorable. They were dressed very "biker chic," and no surprise, several of the men watched them a little obsessively.

"Oh my gosh, guys, you look great," I said, and hugged them.

"There are some hot pieces of ass here," Jasmine said looking around.

I shook my head and laughed. "You're insane."

"Well, she's right," Parker said. "I might not have put it quite that way, but she's not wrong."

"Where's Dash?" Jasmine asked.

I looked around, but couldn't see him. "I don't know."

Arms wrapped around me from behind and Dash said, "Right here, baby."

I giggled and craned my head to kiss him quickly. "Sneak."

Dash released me to hug my friends and then we introduced them to a few key people, including Gator and Doc.

Levi arrived a few minutes later, then the rest of the night was spent getting to know the men, women, and kids of the club. I fell in love with pretty much everyone in the room and found myself never wanting to leave.

After dinner, we sat at a picnic table, Dash on the table, me on the bench between his legs. He leaned down and kissed my temple and I craned my neck to smile up at him.

"You want a beer?"

I shook my head. "Water?"

"Sure, babe, I'll grab you one."

"Thanks."

He maneuvered around me and jumped down, heading off to the cooler with the drinks. Jasmine scooted closer to me and slipped her hand in the crook of my arm. "I really like him."

I grinned. "I really like him, too."

"Yeah?"

"I love him, actually."

Jasmine settled her head on my shoulder. "I'm really glad, honey. I hate Brad."

I giggled. "I know you do."

"Oh, no, I hid my level of disgust for the man."

"Newsflash: No, you didn't," I countered.

She sighed. "Well, I tried."

I raised an eyebrow in challenge.

"What? I did! Do you know how many times I wanted to kick him in the nuts and I *didn't?*" she asked. "I should get some sort of award."

"I will buy you a leg lamp."

She grinned. "I know exactly where I can put it."

"You're ridiculous," I breathed out. "But I love you more than life itself."

Jasmine sat up and turned toward a couple by another one of the burn barrels. "Parker's getting cozy."

"I see that."

"Do you know the guy?"

"No. I'll have to ask Dash about him." I faced her. "What about you?"

"No one I'm digging just yet, but I hope I'll be allowed to come again and check out any prospects I might find."

"You're always welcome here, Jazz," Dash said, handing me a bottled water.

She grinned. "I like you more and more every day."

"Ditto, babe."

"Okay, gotta save Parker and then pee," she said as she stood.

"Don't think your girl needs savin'," Dash said.

"I'm just gonna make sure."

Dash chuckled. "Knock yourself out."

Jasmine walked away and Dash set our drinks on the table and pulled me up.

"What are you…?"

He turned us so our backs were to the group and pulled something out of his pocket.

"Oh, my word, are those my undies?" I whispered.

"Yep." He grinned and dropped them in the barrel. "Was waitin' until we were alone."

"Have you had those in your pocket this entire time?"

"Yeah."

"Well, that's kind of disgusting." I wrapped my arms around his waist and squeezed. "But it also makes you the sweetest man on the planet."

He chuckled, pulling me close. "Don't tell anyone, you'll ruin my reputation."

"Your secret's safe with me." I leaned up and kissed him quickly. "Thanks, honey."

"You bet."

He led me back to the table and we resumed our earlier position and I loved being kind of enclosed in the protectiveness of his body.

"Who's the guy totally into Parker?" I asked.

"Alamo."

"What kind of name is Alamo?"

"He's from Texas."

I looked up at him. "But no one survived the Alamo."

He grinned. "Yeah, that's why his name's ironic. He's never lost a fight."

I thought that was strange, because it seemed like Parker was looking to Jasmine for her blessing. In the end, I chalked it up to Parker being in a new place and making sure her friend was close. Regardless, Parker was always so tight-lipped about her emotions, so I knew I wouldn't get any information out of her until I beat it out of her... face-to-face.

"He's a good guy, baby. Been around a little longer than me and has a past, but he won't hurt her."

"What kind of past?"

"Not my story to tell."

I craned my head to meet his eyes. "A violent past?"

"Babe."

"Surely, you can give me something, Dash. She's my best friend, if she's getting hit on by some psychopath, I should know about it."

He chuckled. "He's not a psychopath. Far from it."

"How far from it."

He kissed me gently. "Not. My. Story."

I wrinkled my nose. "Well, that's dumb."

"You're welcome to ask him."

I gasped. "I would never do that."

"Why not?"

"Because I don't know him and it would be rude."

"Okay, then," Dash murmured. "Want me to introduce you? Then you'll know him...kind of."

"Um, sure." I rose to my feet, turning to face him. "But first I want to make out a little."

He grinned, pulling me close. "I wanna do more than make out."

"Me too," I admitted. "But you'll just have to make up for it tonight."

"I can do that."

He kissed me like I was the most precious thing on earth and then we got interrupted, so we used that distraction to meet a few more people. Alamo was incredibly sweet, although, I found it strange he kept staring at Jasmine while chatting with Parker. I figured I'd never really understand the way of the alpha male.

I met Doom, who was the one of the road captains. He was super standoffish, but nice. There was Rabbit, a recruit who had been gone all week on something Dash called 'a run,' and he was standing with a man by the name of Otter whose smile lit up his whole face.

Dash's friends were some of the most genuine people I'd ever met and I was liking them better than most of the people I'd known for a lifetime.

I said as much when Dash and I headed to bed just before two.

"You're amazin', baby, you know that?"

I switched off the bathroom light and joined him in the bedroom. "What do you mean?"

He was sitting on the edge of the bed, so I stepped between his legs. He grinned up at me. "You've been raised to believe a certain way, embraced your beliefs wholeheartedly, but when you found out something that was counter to what you were led to believe, you made up your own mind without judgement."

I smiled, stroking his cheeks. "I kind of hold to the part in the Bible where we shouldn't judge."

"But a lot don't." He slid his hands up my hips. "Just think you're amazing, is all."

I grinned, leaning down to kiss him. "Well, you've kind of shown me a very different side than what I was led to believe, so that's partly you too, you know."

"Maybe it's the magic of us."

I giggled. "You are so romantic."

"Yeah, you kind of make me that way too."

I kissed him and found myself flipped on my back and his mouth moving down my body. He unclasped my bra and tugged it down my arms and I slid my hands into his hair as he drew a nipple into his mouth and bit down gently.

I arched against him as he continued to shower attention on my breasts while sliding a hand under the waistband of my panties and between my legs. His finger slid through the wetness and then slipped inside of me. I groaned and pushed against him again as he slid another inside. His thumb found my clit and I moaned. I could feel my orgasm building, but before it washed over me, he removed his hand, and stood.

"Where are you going?"

He pushed his jeans from his hips and I grinned. Good Lord, he was pretty. After he slid my panties from my hips, he slid on a condom and rose up above me, settling his hips between mine and guiding himself inside of me. I wrapped my legs around him and arched up.

"Fuck, baby." He slid out of me and then back in slowly. "God, you feel so good."

"More, honey."

He covered my mouth with his and thrust deep inside of me.

"Yes," I whispered against his lips.

His tongue slid into my mouth as his cock surged deeper and deeper, faster and faster. I broke the kiss and moaned. "Dash!" I called out.

I felt my orgasm build and relished the feeling, but when his hand slid between us and his finger found my clit, it was over and I exploded around him. I screamed out his name again as I gripped his biceps and tried to catch my breath.

Within seconds, I felt Dash pulsate inside of me and he kissed my neck as he rolled us onto our sides. "I'll make that last a little longer next time."

"I can see why women choose to fall."

He laughed, kissing my chin. "God, I love you, Willow."

"Love you too." I looped my arms around his neck and

wove my fingers in his hair. "I hope you have a *lot* of condoms."

He met my eyes. "Yeah, baby. I have enough." He smiled and kissed me before sliding out of me and heading to the bathroom. "I'm getting tested next week."

I leaned up on my forearms. "For?"

He returned and stood at the edge of the bed wrapping his hands around my thighs. "For everything. You on the pill?"

"No. Wait, tested? Why would you need to be tested? Did you have a scare?"

"No. I'm always gloved, baby. But I figured if we want to have fun ungloved, you'd want to know I'm clean."

"Gosh, I didn't even think about that." I sighed. "I'm venturing into territory here that I have no experience in."

"I'll be your tour guide, baby, don't worry."

He pulled my body down the bed, causing me to fall onto my back again, and sliding my legs over his shoulders. "You should get on the pill though."

"Um, okay. I might need to find a different doctor. Mine goes to my church and I'm not really ready to open that can yet."

"You can come with me to the clinic. They can do it all there."

I nodded. "Okay, that would be good."

I shifted as his mouth kissed his way down the inside of my left thigh. "Don't move."

I took a deep breath and bit my lip, dropping my head back to the mattress. He lowered his mouth to my clit and sucked until I couldn't help myself from bucking my hips. He gripped my thighs tighter and lowered my bottom to the bed, spreading my knees. I whimpered as he sucked harder, slipping a finger inside of me. I slid my hand into his hair and arched against his mouth.

Without warning, he stood, pulling me further down

the bed, and slammed into me. I cried out and arched again.

"Too much, baby?" he asked.

I shook my head, arching into him again. "No. I want more."

He grasped my thighs again, holding them against his hips and lifting me slightly as he surged into me. I fisted my hands in the comforter, somewhat unable to do much else because Dash held me tight to his body. He thrust into me again and again and I cried out as I came around him. He followed soon after and then held me for a few minutes before getting rid of the condom.

I let my body fall to the mattress, my legs nothing but jelly, and smiled as he returned to the bed. "Oh, my word."

He laughed and stretched out beside me, pulling me into his arms. "You like that?"

I nuzzled his neck and sighed. "I can honestly say, I never thought sex would be like this. You've transported me to a completely different level."

"I aim to please."

"You do. All the time."

He chuckled. "Good to know."

* * *

TWO DAYS LATER, Dash surprised me with a trip into Savannah, well, just outside of Savannah, to take care of our personal business and then we headed to Tybee Island for two days of just us. He had Jazz pack for me, so I had no idea what I'd find until we got to the hotel. Knowing my best friend, I was anticipating crotchless panties, a bikini, and not much more.

We checked into a hotel right on the beach and headed up to our room overlooking the water. Dash had reserved a large room with a king-sized bed and I walked to the sliding glass door and opened it, taking in the view of the beach from our little balcony.

He wrapped an arm around my waist and kissed my temple. "Beach, pool, or bed?"

I giggled. "Food. I need food."

"Order in or go out?"

"Out."

He grinned. "Let's go explore."

We left the room and walked the beach for a bit, then found a kitschy crab place where we stuffed ourselves, before heading back to the room.

"I can't move," I said, flopping onto the bed. "I ate too much."

Dash stretched out beside me. "That's because you ate twice as much as I did."

"Hush."

"Are you disagreeing with me?"

"No, but you should never discuss the amount a lady eats."

He chuckled. "Forgive me, my lady."

"We forgive you," I said, using the queenly "we." I grinned. "Feel like a swim?"

"How about a hot tub?"

"I can get behind that…*if* Jazz packed my swimsuit."

"I told her to," he said, as he slid off the bed and dropped my suitcase onto it. "I also told her to pack a little black dress and those boots of yours I love."

I sat up and raised an eyebrow. "She knew which boots to pack? I own more than a few."

He grinned, pulling out the boots in question. "She sure did."

I clapped my hands. "Well done, Jasmine."

I joined him at my bag and pulled out everything Jasmine had packed. Of course, she picked the bikini I'd never worn (partly because it was a little too small and a little too revealing), but it was all I had, so I had no choice but to go with it. I grabbed a T-shirt out of the bag to wear over it, so at least I had some semblance of modesty.

Dash, however, tugged it from my hands.

"Hey," I snapped. "Give that back."

"Huh-uh, I wanna see you in that first."

"I have no problem with you seeing me in it," I said. "But it's really revealing."

"Put it on."

I rolled my eyes and stripped before shimmying the bikini on. Dash growled, lifting me onto the bed and hovering over me. "Dash!"

"Yeah, you're gonna wear the T-shirt," he said, pushing the top up over my breasts. "But first…"

I sighed as he sucked a nipple into his mouth and bit down gently. The bikini bottoms tied on the sides, so he tugged them loose and the material fell away. He didn't waste any time moving to my core where his tongue slid inside of me, then he moved to my clit.

"Dash," I rasped.

Dropping his jeans to the floor, he kicked them away, ripped open a condom packet and put it on faster than he ever had, then pushed into me. I arched to get closer with a whimper.

"Beautiful, baby. So fuckin' beautiful."

I linked my fingers with his and kissed his neck. "I love you."

"Love you more, Willow."

He slammed into me and my orgasm hit a little too fast for my liking, but he made me come once more before letting himself go. He kissed me gently before sliding out of me and heading to the bathroom. "Can't wait to get rid of these fuckin' condoms."

I giggled. "Is it much better without it?"

He returned with a washcloth and cleaned me up. "Never done it ungloved, but I've heard it's a million times better."

"Pretty sure if it gets any better, I'll combust."

Dash chuckled. "You're good for my ego."

I shrugged. "I'm just pointing out the things you do right...if you stop doing that, we'll have a different conversation."

He grinned, leaning down to kiss me again. "Fair enough."

"I'm really going to need that hot tub now. I think you killed my vagina."

Dash dropped his head back and laughed. "I haven't even begun to kill your vagina. Ten days and I'll be able to show you bareback"

I giggled. "Bring it."

We redressed and headed down to the pool.

* * *

THE NEXT MORNING, I rolled over and snuggled closer to Dash, kissing his bare chest and then climbing out of bed to check out the view.

"Where are you goin'?" he asked, his hair a mess, his eyes sleepy as he blinked a few times, then ran his hands down his face.

"It's raining," I said, peeking out the slider. "It's gorgeous."

"Weirdo. Come back to bed and keep me warm."

"Come and see how pretty the rain is," I countered.

He chuckled, pushing up from the mattress. "Damn it, woman, it's freezing."

"I'll warm you, you big baby, but come look at the view."

Dash stalked his gloriously naked body to me, wrapping his arms around me, and pulling me against him. "It's pretty. Come back to bed."

"Lordy, you remind me of Clark Griswold looking at the Grand Canyon." I nodded toward the ocean. "Enjoy it for a second."

He sighed and stared out at the view again...for at least

eight seconds this time, and then he turned me to face him and smiled. "You're prettier."

I cocked my head in challenge. "Prettier than the Grand Canyon?"

"Yes. And the ocean under the rain or the sun or whatever." He kissed me. "Not just because you're gorgeous. But because your soul is perfect and you make me watch the rain on the ocean. You're right, it's beautiful, and sometimes I miss shit, but you make me stop and notice it."

"Dash," I whispered, blinking back tears.

"I love you, Willow. I love everything about you." He kissed me again. "Thank you for making me stop and look at the beauty around me."

I looped my arms around his neck and held him tight. "You are so unbelievably sweet, do you know that?"

"Only to you."

"I'm the only one here right now." I grinned. "But I know you're sweet a lot. Don't worry, I won't tell."

He chuckled, leaning down to kiss me.

"I kind of don't want to go home," I admitted.

"Right there with you, baby."

"I have to meet with my advisor in two weeks to finalize classes, but I'd like to pretend we're on vacation until then."

Dash chuckled. "I'll figure out how to do that."

"You will?"

"Yep. Maybe I'll keep you naked for the next two weeks."

I giggled. "So, it's all about you...I get it."

"Hey, you love it too."

"You're right." I stroked his face. "I really, really do."

"I'm gonna give you a little something you won't forget, *then* we'll get back to the real world, sound good?"

I grinned. "So good."

THIRTEEN

Willow

THE NEXT DAY, Dash took me home and as we attempted to make dinner, I couldn't seem to stop touching him. Apparently, this got him a little hot and bothered. "You like rilin' me up?" he asked as he cupped my breast.

"Very much so."

"You want more?" he asked.

I licked my lips and nodded. My breasts felt heavy and my nipples pebbled into tight buds. He slid his hand under my T-shirt, cupping my breasts as he kissed me. After he was done there, he yanked my jeans down my legs and dragged his fingers through my wetness.

"Soaked, baby," he whispered as he thumbed my clit, then shoved two fingers inside of me.

"You make me this way," I panted out.

"Don't you forget it." He tugged my T-shirt off, and removed my bra, then turned me to face the kitchen island, and splayed his palm across my belly as he slid his other hand between my legs. "So fuckin' ready."

I licked my lips and moaned as he fingered my wetness and then slid two fingers inside of me again. Keeping his fingers inside of me, he pressed gently on my back. "Hold onto the counter, baby."

I leaned forward and did as he directed, swallowing as he slid into me from behind. "Lower," he ordered.

The cold granite against my nipples was incredible. I moaned as he pushed me further against the cold.

"Feel good?" he asked.

"Yes. So, so good."

He grabbed my hips and buried himself inside of me, eliciting an orgasm before we'd even really gotten started. Good Lord, he was the *master*.

He didn't stop for me to catch my breath or relish my climax, just pulled out slightly, then surged back into me, and I braced again as he continued to thrust faster and faster. I dropped my head, my body having a difficult time staying upright.

His hand slid to my clit again and I cried out as another orgasm overtook me. He wasn't far behind and covered my back with his body as he pulsed inside of me.

Lifting me gently, he slid out of me. "Fuck, baby. Just gets better."

I leaned back against the counter in order to keep myself upright. "My legs feel like Jell-O."

Dash chuckled. "Need me to carry you to the bathroom to clean up?"

I smiled. "I'm pretty sure I can handle that."

"Gonna get rid of the condom, then I'm makin' you

dinner."

While he cleaned up, I put my clothes back on and washed my hands, then we went about finally making dinner.

* * *

A FEW HOURS later, we decided to call it a night...mostly because it was another exercise in constant touching and riling Dash up. As we crossed the threshold of my bedroom, he covered my mouth with his, lifting me so I could wrap my legs around his waist. Our kiss was a desperate connecting of tongues and hands and lips as he carried me to the mattress. I wove my hands into his hair and tugged gently as he settled me on the bed and slid my shirt up.

Popping the front hook on my bra, he cupped my breasts, running my nipples between his fingertips as he gently sucked each one into his mouth. I lost his mouth when he stood, pulling his shirt over his head, but since the sight of him shirtless was beautiful, I didn't mind.

I didn't think I'd ever get sick of seeing him naked. Goodness, he was gorgeous. Smooth chest, tattoos, muscles on muscles—I couldn't help but lick my lips as he removed the rest of his clothes, and after he'd divested me of the rest of mine, crawled into the bed beside me.

He grinned, leaning down to kiss me, and then moving his way down my body, his face disappearing between my legs. I whimpered when his mouth connected with my clit, sucking it gently. I fisted my hands in the sheets and arched against him.

"Dash, I...I'm...I can't wait."

He didn't respond verbally... just put more pressure on my core with his tongue. I anchored my heels to his shoulders and bit my lip, trying to keep my climax at bay. I couldn't. I cried out, my body shaking as I came.

Dash kissed the inside of my thighs then hovered over me and slid inside. I moaned with need, the feel of him almost too much. Linking his fingers with mine, he dragged them over my head and buried himself deeper in my body as he licked my bottom lip and then kissed me deeply. I slid a leg over his hip and arched into him.

I sighed against his mouth. "I love everything about this."

He grinned. "Wanna try something new?"

"Yes," I answered immediately.

Dash released my hands and slid out of me. "On your knees, baby."

"My knees?"

"Yeah, baby, I'll walk you through it."

I rolled over and pushed up on all fours as he directed.

"You good like this, or do you want a pillow under your hips?" he asked.

"I have no idea," I admitted.

Dash squeezed my bottom as he slid back inside me, and I let out a quiet squeak.

"You okay?" Dash asked.

"Oh, my word, yes, this is amazing."

"Need a pillow?"

"No."

He pushed in again, reaching one of his hands to a breast and the other to my clit. He worked my body until I could barely breathe, and then he grabbed my hips and slammed into me over and over again until I cried out, collapsing onto the mattress. Dash fell with me, rolling us onto our sides so he could continue to slam into me.

"Dash, I'm going to come again."

"Wait," he growled.

I whimpered, unsure I'd be able to do what he demanded.

"Now, baby," he rasped, and his body locked.

I let myself go and contracted around him as he kissed the nape of my neck. "I love you, Willow."

"I love you, too."

He slid out of me, got rid of the condom, and brought a washcloth to clean me up.

I snuggled against him. "Thank you."

"No problem, baby. Now I'm gonna sleep, yeah? Unless you need my dick a little more."

I giggled. "I'm good...for a little while."

He pulled me close and I fell asleep...fast.

* * *

Dash

TWO DAYS LATER, I walked into the compound and back to Doc's office. I'd left Willow in her bed with Gator downstairs on watch. She wasn't happy that I'd woken her to tell her Gator was on her sofa, but I figured she'd be even more pissed if she'd walked downstairs in nothin' but panties and T-shirt.

"Hey, brother," Badger said, giving me a nod.

"Hey, man, what'd you find?"

"I'm not sure exactly what kind of shit you've stepped into Dash, but I can tell you that it's pretty fuckin' deep." This came from Rabbit, our resident computer whiz, who could run circles around Booker.

"What do you mean?" I asked.

"These Torrance Group assholes are big time," Badger said. "From what we can see, there are three major players involved, all local to Savannah, and all heavily invested, as in *tens of millions* each."

I let out a slow whistle.

Rabbit nodded. "All the names are encoded, so we still don't have all the details, but I can tell you these guys have been buying up local real estate like crazy over the past six months, and for pennies on the dollar."

"Why?" I frowned. "And how are they getting the land for so cheap?"

"That's what we're trying to figure out," Badger said.

"But from what they did to Willow's dad, I'm gonna assume these guys prefer the stick over the carrot when it comes to business negotiations."

"How did Alfred get wrapped up in big-time land deals and killers?"

"We haven't figured it all out yet, but we think these entries here have to do with the church," Rabbit pointed to a column on the spreadsheet, "and that these figures here are offers they made to him. Alfred was smart, Dash. He's been tracking these guys for a while now."

"Then it's a really good thing we found this information before they did."

"I'm not so sure about that," Badger said.

"Why not?"

"The shit in this file obviously got Alfred killed. Once they find out we have it, they'll come after us. Who knows who these guys are and how much muscle they have."

"Sounds like you'd better find out who they are, and fast."

"Yeah, and you need to keep Willow close."

"Don't worry about that...I got her."

"I'm sending this shit back to Booker," Rabbit said. "He's gonna dig deeper, so we stay off these assholes' radar."

"Let me take it first. I'm going to see if any of this makes sense to Willow."

"Are you sure you want to get her involved any deeper?" Badger asked.

"How much deeper could she be, Badger? They've already killed her father, and they'd kill her if they knew she was there when it happened."

"Just be careful."

"Thanks, brother." I grinned. "You guys' comin' for dinner?"

"Yeah, man," Badger said. "Can't turn down food that doesn't come from a microwave."

"I'll need to take a raincheck," Rabbit said. "Doom's got me doin' some shit."

I chuckled. "See ya later, then."

* * *

Willow

"WHATYA COOKIN', BABY girl?" Gator asked, from his place on the sofa.

"I'm roasting a chicken."

"Smells delicious."

"Yeah?" I retorted, setting some potatoes on the island. "Wanna come over here and peel some potatoes?"

"Do I look like I got tits?"

I raised an eyebrow. "I don't really think you want me to answer that, old man."

He glanced down, roared with laughter, then stood and made his way to the kitchen. "Give me the damn peeler."

I handed it to him like a nurse would hand a scalpel to a doctor and he laughed again, but sat his butt on a stool and began to peel.

The doorbell rang and I moved toward it, but Gator stopped me. "You don't answer the door, baby girl, you know that."

I rolled my eyes. "It's probably Dash."

"Dash has a key."

I bit my lip. He was right. Dash *did* have a key and he would never ring the doorbell. Gator went to the door and I followed, but hung back a bit.

"Who the fuck are you?" Gator growled.

"I'm Willow's fiancé," Brad snapped back.

"Willow don't got a fiancé," Gator replied. "She's got a man, but it sure as shit ain't you."

I sighed and decided to cut this off at the pass. "It's okay, Gator. I know him."

"But I don't."

I squeezed his arm. "He's my *ex*-fiancé, it's fine."

It took a minute, but he stepped aside and I moved to the door. "What can I do for you, Brad?"

"Can I come in?" he asked. "Or are you going to make me stand on the porch like a salesman."

I heard a low growl come from Gator and sighed. "I don't think it would be a good idea for you to come in. What do you need?"

"Can't a man check up on the woman he loves after her father's murdered?"

I swallowed. Leave it to Brad to use "murdered" instead of maybe "death" or "passing," or something that wouldn't be a direct hit to my heart. "I'm sorry, Brad, but that's not really appropriate…now that you and I have *broken up.*"

He sighed. "I'd hoped you might have come to your senses by now."

"Come to my *senses*?"

"You're *mine*, Willow. We had a deal, but instead you're prostituting yourself out to these…these low-life biker assholes?"

Before I could respond, I was gently moved out of the doorway and Gator shoved Brad, and then hit him so hard, he fell back, flat on his butt.

"What the fuck did you call her?" Gator bellowed.

The roar of pipes got closer and closer as Gator continued to hit Brad, and I continued to try and stop him, then Dash was there and physically pulling Gator off an extremely bruised and battered politician's son.

"Gate…stop, man, fuck!" Dash snapped.

"The motherfucker called Willow a whore."

Dash released Gator. "What the fuck?"

I gasped. "Gator!"

"You called Willow a whore?" Dash seethed, his hands now fisted at his sides.

"Ignore him." I rushed to him and grabbed his arm.

"Come inside."

"Apologize, asshole," Dash demanded.

"Apologize? He broke my tooth!" Brad cried out. Blood was now pouring from his mouth and his right eye was already swelling shut.

"You're lucky he didn't do a lot more."

"Just ignore him, Dash," I begged.

Dash ignored me, looming over Brad again. "Apologize."

"We need to get him a doctor," I argued.

"I didn't hit him hard enough for him to need a doctor," Gator countered.

I frowned at him, then looked at Brad. He sure looked like Gator hit him hard enough to need a doctor to me, so I moved to help, but Dash took my arm and pulled me back. "Go inside, Willow."

"I can't leave him bleeding on my lawn, Dash. I need to help him."

Dash scowled, then focused on Brad. "You need an ambulance, asshole?"

Brad dabbed at his lip with the handkerchief he'd pulled from his blazer pocket. "No, but you're gonna need a lawyer."

"Brad. Are you really okay?" I asked.

"Willow, go in the house," Dash ordered.

"Not until I know he's okay."

I was watching Brad closely, but Dash's chest appeared in front of me and I was forced to look up at him.

"Go inside, baby," he repeated. "I'll take care of this."

"Please don't let him leave here if he's really hurt. I don't want Gator to get in trouble," I whispered, and Dash grinned. "Why are you smiling?"

"Give me a minute to deal with this and I'll tell you."

I wrinkled my nose. "If you're not in the house in five minutes, I'm coming back out here."

Dash glanced over my head and then Gator was virtually carrying me back inside.

FOURTEEN

Dash

I WAITED UNTIL I heard the locks on the door click, then I faced Brad and crossed my arms. The asshole had managed to pick himself up off the ground, but he was hurtin', and that made me feel somewhat elated...I just wish I'd been the one to hit him.

"What do you want with her?" Brad demanded.

I cocked my head. "I need you to be more specific."

"You want her money?"

"What money?"

I assumed he was talking about the insurance policy, but the fact he knew about it didn't sit well with me.

"She obviously hasn't told you, which leads me to believe..."

"What does it lead you to believe, asshole?"

He chuckled, still holding a rag on his lip. "She'll come to her senses and set you aside as soon as she realizes I'm the right man for her."

"Ya think?"

"She'll regret it if she doesn't."

"You come anywhere near her again, you'll be pickin' up more than your teeth off the ground. Now, fuck off, asshole," I snapped, and walked back into the house.

I locked the door, reset the alarm, and then headed into the kitchen. Willow stood at the island chopping vegetables and she seemed off. "Willow?"

"Hmm?" she murmured without looking up.

"No kiss hello?" I challenged.

She set the knife down, walked over to me, and gave me a quick kiss on the lips, then immediately went back to what she was doing. I frowned. "Babe, what's goin' on?"

"I'm goin' to go out back and grab a smoke," Gator said, making himself scarce.

"Willow?"

She shook her head and focused on the veggies again.

I sighed, closing the distance between us and carefully prying the knife out of her hand. "Talk to me."

She dropped her head to my chest. "I just...feel...I don't know...like an errant child."

"In what way?"

"You wouldn't understand."

Admittedly, this irritated me a little. "Try me."

"Brad accused me of prostituting myself—"

"Stop," I growled.

"I knew you wouldn't understand."

I lifted her chin. "Okay, first, fuck Brad and the horse he rode in on. Second, you are not a whore, but you know what? Even if you were, he'd have no right to judge you. And believe me, baby, that asshole's probably got more skeletons in his closet than he's willing to admit." She bit her lip and I kissed her gently. "You're perfect just the way you are, Willow. Don't ever doubt it."

"I appreciate that. But it's just hard to dismiss those bits in the Bible that say premarital sex is wrong."

"You love me?"

"So, so much," she whispered.

"You ever want to fuck Brad?"

Her face screwed up into the cutest expression of disgust and I had to force myself not to smile. "No, I didn't even enjoy his kisses...I mean, I guess I did back then, but now that I've kissed you, I realize he kind of sucked at it."

I chuckled, kissing her again. "I'm gonna make an honest woman outta you, Willow, so don't listen to the people who want to drag you down."

She grinned, wrapping her arms around my waist. "Thanks, honey."

"It's all good."

"Are you okay with the whole Brad thing?"

"Why wouldn't I be okay?"

She shrugged, going back to her veggies. "He can be mean."

I grabbed a beer from the fridge. "I can handle douchebag Brad."

"Will you tell me why you were giggly before?"

"Giggly?" I challenged.

"Oh, sorry, that's not very manly, huh?" she retorted. "The part where you said you'd tell me inside."

"I know what you were talkin' about, baby, just like to give you a hard time."

She rolled her eyes.

"You said you didn't want Gator to get in trouble. You

put his well-being before Brad's."

"Well, yeah." She waved the knife in the air. "I don't want a repeat of what happened when you and I met."

"For the second time."

"I wasn't sure if you remembered that."

I cocked my head. "Not remember the fuckin' hot piece of ass who got her back up 'cause she wanted to change her own tire?"

"I didn't 'get my back up,' I just didn't know you and you were really gorgeous, and that made me all nervous."

I kissed her again. "Glad you don't get nervous anymore."

"Oh, I do, I'm just better at hiding it."

I laughed. "You hide it well."

Gator walked in just as the oven timer started to beep.

"Timer's goin' off," Gator retorted, parking himself back on a bar stool.

"You want to chop more veggies, old man?" Willow threatened, turning off the timer.

Gator chuckled. "I'm happy to chop veggies if you feed me like this every night. I ain't never had better food in my life than when you cook."

Willow beamed. "You're a boost to a girl's ego, Gator."

I wrapped an arm around her waist and kissed her temple. "You need help?"

"Do you know how to set a table?"

"Probably not the way you want it."

"Love how honest you are." She smiled. "How about you watch the veggies and turn them when the timer goes off? I'll set the table."

"I can do that."

Willow instructed Gator on what she wanted carried to the dining room and left me standing at the stove. Lucky for her, I could cook...not like she could, but enough to know what turning the veggies meant.

* * *

Willow

I LOVED DASH. More than anything, but I couldn't seem to get the little insecurities that filled my mind to disappear. The biggest problem was that I was a verbal processor and we were hosting our friends tonight, so I wouldn't be able to break it all down until they were gone.

So, I shut down a little. This wasn't like me, but it was all I could do in order to keep myself from completely losing my mind.

Badger and Alamo arrived first and made themselves comfortable while Dash grabbed them beer. Jasmine and Parker walked in not long after, and they'd brought wine and dessert, which sent me looking for the wine opener. I hadn't had a decent glass of wine all week and I suddenly needed it.

"Can we help?" Jasmine asked.

"Nope. I'm pretty much done."

She cocked her head and studied me. "You got a second?"

I was mid-sip into my wine, so I swallowed and nodded.

Jasmine headed toward my dad's office and I followed, closing the door as I stepped inside. "What's up?" I asked.

She crossed her arms. "What's wrong?"

"What do you mean? I'm good."

"You're a shit liar, little miss, spill."

Because it was Jasmine, and because she was impossible to stall, lie to, bamboozle, or accomplish anything shady involving her, I told her everything. Brad's visit and all of my insecurities and feelings about Dash and sex...all of it.

"Okay, give me a second to process the fact you've lost your V-card," she said, with a cheeky grin.

"Jasmine," I hissed.

She giggled. "I think it's awesome."

"That's because you like sex."

"Well, that's true. I do like sex. But it's not like I've slept with a hundred men or anything."

I rolled my eyes. "I know that."

She'd had two serious boyfriends in her life and made a (very loud) point of waiting seven months and two days (she was a total weirdo like that), and if she was in love by that date in the relationship, she'd have sex. Two men had made the cut, and she'd just broken up with Wally, so the clock would start again when she met a new man.

"And I get where you're coming from with the sex before marriage and everything, but I think what you have with Dash is realer than what you had with Brad, and realer than what a lot of couples have, period. He's good for you, Willow. Really good for you."

"I know he is."

"So, do you really think God is concerned about a piece of paper? In Biblical times, they had sex first and the ceremony after, so if you marry him, you're kind of covered, right?"

"What if I don't marry him?"

She grinned. "Oh, then you're definitely a whore and you're going to hell."

I sighed. "Thanks, butthead."

Jasmine giggled. "You're welcome. Feel better?"

"Much."

"Good," she said. "And, F.Y. information, Brad's a dick. He's always been a dick and he'll forever be a dick, so listen to *nothing* he says, got it?"

"Good advice," Dash said from the doorway.

"So, he doesn't knock," Jasmine deadpanned. "Good

to know."

Dash grinned and closed the distance between us.

"I'll give you guys a minute," Jasmine said, and left the room.

"How much did you hear?" I asked.

"Most of it."

"Didn't your mom tell you eavesdropping was rude?"

"Never knew my mom, so no."

I frowned, sliding my hands up his chest. "You didn't know your mom?"

He shook his head. "Nope. She died when I was about two...drug overdose. Was raised by my aunt."

"What about your dad?"

"He was some john she'd fucked to get high."

I frowned. "You were a drug baby?"

"Believe it or not, no. The second she found out she was pregnant, she did everything she could to get sober. But she couldn't stay that way once I was born. My aunt got custody before she OD'd and it was her and me against the world until I was eighteen. She met her husband Tony when I was sixteen, but didn't marry him 'til I was technically an adult. She wanted me to know I was her priority. So, I left and she and her hubs moved to Atlanta about six years ago."

"She kicked you out?"

"No. I took off on my own. She sacrificed a shit ton for me, and I was holding her back, so I packed up and left. I'd met Doc a few months before I turned eighteen and he offered me a place and I never left."

"Do you still see your aunt?"

"Not as much as I'd like to," he admitted. "She's got a couple of kids and her husband's cool, but it's a trek to get there and they're busy."

I wrapped my arms around his waist. "I'm sorry."

"Don't be sorry, baby. My life's good and it's all because of Brooke. We're still tight, it's just distance that makes it difficult."

"I can't wait to meet her."

He grinned. "Can't wait to introduce you two. She's gonna love you."

"You think so?"

"I know so," he said, giving me a gentle squeeze. "I've already told her about you, and now I get a text every couple of days asking when she gets to meet you."

"So, when's that going to happen?"

He chuckled. "Want to go before school starts?"

"Yes."

"I'll set something up." He lifted my chin. "You feel better?"

I nodded. "Yes."

"Good, 'cause Gator wants food."

"Gator *always* wants food."

"This is true." He grinned, leaning down to kiss me gently, then we headed back to our friends.

* * *

EVERYONE WAS GONE and I had rushed to get naked…I needed Dash in a bad, bad way. He was taking a little longer than I liked, but the second he'd slid his jeans off, I knelt in front of him and slid my mouth over the tip of his cock.

"Fuck, Willow. You sure you wanna do this?"

I nodded and smiled as he threaded his fingers into my hair. Admittedly, I had no experience, but I had an idea of what I needed to do and I wanted to do it well. I took him deeper, but my efforts didn't last long. Strong hands hooked me under my arms and I was lifted onto the bed.

"Dash! I'm not—" I never got the rest of my complaint out, as Dash thrust inside of me and all breath left my body with a squeak, "Oh!" It was our first night without condoms and it felt amazing.

His mouth claimed mine as he continued to surge into

me, his hand cupping my breast before sliding between my legs. My orgasm flooded me, but I didn't have time to enjoy it, as I was flipped onto my stomach. "Cheek to the mattress, baby."

My heart raced as I did as he directed. He lifted my hips higher and slid into me from behind and I lost my mind. "Oh, my word," I breathed out.

"Don't come," he ordered.

"I don't think I can control—" Before I'd even gotten the sentence out, I exploded around him again.

Dash groaned, sliding partially out and then back in. "Fuck, baby, so good."

I mewed as another climax began to build.

"I'm gonna try somethin'," Dash said. "You trust me?"

"Yes," I rasped, and he smacked my bottom. I let out a shocked cry, but my body immediately responded.

"Too much?" he asked.

"No. Oh…my…"

"More?"

"Yes, honey. More."

He slapped me gently again and I closed my eyes, my mind and body overwhelmed with pleasure. Dash moved slower, his hands settled on my hips, and I continued to moan as my orgasm built. He shifted slightly, sliding his hand to my belly. "Spread baby."

I spread and he lifted me, keeping himself firmly inside of me, so I was straddling him backwards. I dropped my head back, onto his shoulder and whimpered.

"You okay?"

"Yes," I panted.

With his left arm anchoring me against him, he rolled a nipple between his fingers while his right hand slid between my legs. I rose slightly, then lowered slowly.

"That's right, baby," he whispered, and I raised up again, mewling as I slid back down. "Holy shit," he rasped, and his finger found home.

I called out his name as I came and he pushed me back down and slammed into me, over and over, until he let out a satisfied groan.

"Just gets better," he whispered, rolling us to our sides.

I wanted more, so I reached between my legs as I rocked my hips, dropping my head back against him.

"I've created a monster," he whispered, replacing my hand with his, his finger going straight to my clit and bringing me to yet another perfect orgasm.

"Yes, you have," I agreed once I caught my breath.

He slid out of me and left the room, returning with a warm washcloth to clean me up.

"Even as messy as this might be, it's so much better without a condom."

Dash chuckled. "Hell, yeah it is."

He climbed back into bed and pulled me onto his chest. "Was I okay?"

"You were incredible, baby."

"Then why did you make me stop?"

He sighed. "Because if I didn't, I was gonna come in your mouth. I figured you weren't ready for that." He ran a finger across my lower lip. "For someone who's never done that before, it was amazing and I knew I wouldn't be able to wait." His finger continued down my chest and across my breast, rolling my nipple. I arched into him.

"Dash," I whispered.

His hand slipped between my legs and he kissed my neck. "I love you, Willow." I spread a little so he'd have better access. "More than I could have ever imagined."

"Dash," I whispered again, and he kissed me deeply.

He slid his arm to my waist and rolled with me, landing on his back. I straddled his hips, lifting up slightly as he guided himself inside of me. I lowered myself with a sigh, bracing my hands behind me on his thighs.

"Fuck me, I'm hard again."

I smiled. "Yes, yes you are."

I raised up again and Dash ordered, "Slowly, baby."

I fell forward and kissed his chest. "Killjoy."

Dash's hand went between us, his finger to my clit, and he grinned. "Rock back and forth, baby."

I pressed into his fingers and rocked gently, my hands on his chest, my head back as he brought me to the edge of a cliff, then over. As I came around him, he rolled me onto my back and slammed into me, dragging my thigh up as he thrust in harder.

Yet another orgasm came just before his, and he kissed me as I wrapped my arms around his neck and slid my fingers into his hair.

"Wow," I breathed out as he rolled off me and onto his back.

"We're gettin' married tomorrow."

I giggled. "Are we?"

"Hell, yeah. I'm not lettin' A-Plus pussy get away."

"Excuse me?"

He grinned, facing me and settling his head in his palm. "Somethin' you need to understand about men…"

I faced him, mimicking his pose. "Oh, please enlighten me, sir."

"When a man finds a woman who satisfies him in bed, he doesn't let her go. For any reason."

"Oh, really?"

"Really," he confirmed. "I've been around, I've had my share of pussy, but yours is pure gold, and there's no way in hell—"

"Wait," I interrupted him. "We need to shut this conversation down, because you're starting to irk me."

"Why's that?"

"Because you're diminishing what this is. You're putting me in the same category with all your other 'pu-pu-pussy.'" I slid out of bed and stalked to the bathroom.

Dash followed. "Will—"

"I'm not having this conversation with you," I said,

pushing the door closed.

I started the shower and climbed in. I wasn't in there long before Dash stepped in behind me and I closed my eyes forcing the hurt away.

"I'm sorry," he whispered, kissing the back of my neck. "I was tryin' to be funny and instead sounded like a dick."

I nodded, keeping my head under the spray.

"Baby," he said, turning me to face him. "Don't be mad."

I wiped the water from my eyes. "I'm not mad. I'm hurt."

He frowned. "That's fuckin' worse."

"Then don't relegate me to 'class A' pussy."

"Technically I said 'A-plus pussy' and that it was 'gold.' That's way better than class A."

"Dash," I hissed.

He chuckled. "I'm sorry. Bad joke."

I sighed. "Can we please make it a point *not* to bring up the current rankings of the industry standards of my genitalia? Because it reminds me just how much of it you've had and it makes me feel lacking."

"Baby, you're not lacking, that's what I was trying to say…badly, but true." He pulled me closer. "Fuck, I'm sorry, Willow. Seriously. I've never had this." He lifted my chin. "I might be 'experienced,' so to speak, but *this*, this is new to me. I've never been in love. I don't know what the fuck I'm doin' most of the time, and if I lost you, I'd lose my mind."

"You're not going to lose me," I said, exasperated. "Not over something like this, anyway."

"No?"

"No." I rolled my eyes. "Dash, I love you. Yes, you hurt my feelings, but you've soothed that hurt in your strange and unique way."

He smiled. "Good."

"I'm not going anywhere unless you cheat on me or hurt one of my friends…"

"Which will never happen."

I stroked his cheek. "Good to know."

"I want you to hear me on that, Willow. I will never cheat on you."

"I hear you, honey, and I believe you."

"And I won't ever intentionally hurt one of your friends."

"Mostly Parker," I said. "Jasmine'll kick your butt if you offend her…she can take care of herself."

He laughed. "Good to know."

"Actually, Parker would probably kick your butt too, she'd just do it really quietly."

"I'll watch my back, then."

"That'd be good."

"I'm sorry for bein' a dick, baby."

I smiled. "I know. It's okay."

He kissed me. "You forgive me?"

"Of course I forgive you." I kissed him. "Like I could stay mad at you." I squeezed his face, making his lips pucker. "This face is irresistible."

He chuckled, leaning down to kiss me again. The kiss turned heated (no surprise there), and he made up for being a 'dick' in the most delicious way possible.

By the time we went back to bed, I couldn't keep my eyes open, and once I snuggled up to my man, I fell asleep almost immediately.

FIFTEEN

Willow

AN ANNOYING RINGING dissonance tried to worm its way into my dream and I wanted none of it. Luckily it stopped and I pulled the covers further over my head.

"Baby, your phone's ringin'."

I groaned, flipping the comforter off my face. "I was *ignoring* it."

Dash reached over me and handed me the subject of my irritation. "Yeah, but whoever it is keeps callin', so you might want to answer it."

"Hello?"

"Turn on your television," Jasmine ordered.

"Why?"

"Ohmigod, Willow, just turn on the news...any news. Brad got arrested."

I sat up with a gasp. "What?"

"What's wrong?" Dash asked.

"Brad got arrested."

"No shit?"

"What channel, Jazz?" I asked, grabbing my remote.

"Any of them. It's breaking news."

"Okay, I'll call you back."

I dropped my phone on the bed and turned on the TV. Flipping through channels, I stopped on the one that flashed Brad's "mugshot" on the screen.

"Brad Aljets, eldest son of Deputy Mayor Percy Aljets, was arrested early Thursday morning on several charges of solicitation of prostitution."

I turned up the volume, not fully believing what I was hearing.

"Mr. Aljets was arrested at a local underground sex club in the early hours of the morning. His arrest comes as a part of an ongoing police investigation of prostitution and drug trafficking in the area. Allegedly, police became aware of Mr. Aljets' involvement when compromising video of several of his "sessions" with a woman known as "Madame Viola Paine" was posted online, as well as sent to a detective at Savannah Chatham Metro. Mr. Aljets has been released on bond. We'll report further details as we get them. Now, for this week's weather forecast...do you have some sunshine for us, John?"

I muted the volume and Dash laughed out loud as he slid off the bed and headed to the bathroom. I was still sitting in stunned silence when he returned and sat beside me again, scrolling through his phone. "Fuck me."

"What?" I asked, jarred out of my shock fog.

"I don't think you wanna see this."

"See what?"

"Brad's compromising video."

I gasped. "You found it?"

He chuckled, then screwed up his face in disgust. "Holy shit, he was into some weird fuckin' shit."

"Like what?"

"No," Dash said, holding the screen to his chest. "Trust me when I say, once you see this, you can never unsee it."

"Show me."

"Baby, will you trust me on this? I don't want your head polluted with this shit."

"How bad could it be?"

"Giant dildo in the shape of a fist ramming up his ass kind of bad."

I covered my face with my hands and tried desperately not to laugh out loud because I was both disgusted and amused by this. "He did not."

"He absolutely did, wearing a dog collar and a ball gag."

"What's a ball gag?"

He groaned. "No, I can't, Willow. I just can't."

I grabbed my phone and looked it up, and immediately wished I hadn't. I dropped my phone back on the bed and covered my mouth with my hand, forcing down the bile.

"I wish you hadn't done that."

"Me too," I admitted.

"Will you trust me next time?"

I bobbed my head emphatically. "Absolutely."

He set his phone on the nightstand. "How much did you investigate?"

I shuddered. "Just the ball gag thingy…that was enough."

I gagged a little and Dash laughed. "Yeah, I'd imagine it would be."

I bit my lip and stared at him for a second.

"What?"

"Have you ever…?"

"Been into someone fisting me? Hell, no."

I giggled. "Is that what it's called?"

"Let's drop this subject, yeah? I've never been into fisting, never paid for sex, and I'm only open to kinky shit if *you* ever want to try it, but fisting's off the table."

I fell onto the mattress, unable to keep myself from laughing. "Oh, my word, now I can't get the visual of me shoving my fist up your butt out of my head."

His hands slid to my waist and he hovered over me. "You think fistin's funny, huh?"

"A little, yeah."

He squeezed and I was so shocked by it, I choked out a laugh.

"Dash!" I squealed.

He continued to tickle me until I could barely breathe. "I'm gonna pee."

"Don't wet the bed, baby."

"Oh, my word, Dash, stop!"

He did immediately, leaning down to kiss me gently. "You're so fuckin' gorgeous when you're laughin'."

"Hold that thought, honey, I really do need to pee."

He grinned, rolling onto his back and I headed to the bathroom. As I washed my face and brushed my teeth, my shock about Brad wore off and my stomach dropped. I realized I'd been engaged to a stranger...even though we'd known each other for years. On the flipside of that, I'd known Dash for a little more than a month and I knew him, knew him. I had no doubts about him, or us, and I trusted him completely.

Brad had said some really nasty things about Dash and I honestly felt like driving down to the jail and punching him. I hated his hypocrisy. I understood that it was something everyone did, and it was often done by people in the church more than most, but I always tried to be transparent, and so did my father. It was how I'd been raised and I chose friends who I believed were honest with me. I'd been so, so wrong about Brad, and it made me feel like an idiot.

"You spiralin'?" Dash asked from the doorway.

I jumped a little as I faced him. "No."

"Really?"

"No."

He chuckled. "You freakin' out a little?"

"A lotta little," I admitted.

He cupped my neck. "Break it down for me."

I filled him in on my thoughts and insecurities and he listened to all of it...without speaking, which was extremely odd for him. But he waited for me to finish and then wrapped his arms around me and pulled me against him. "Okay, first, and I seriously can't believe I'm fuckin' havin' to say this, but you're not an idiot. You trust people. That's not being an idiot, it's being kind."

I leaned against him, letting my body fall into his.

"Second, all of us...your people, my people...tend to view people through our own filter. You don't lie and you live by a code of transparency, so you believe others do as well. That's also not being an idiot. Your way is the right way, so don't let that asshole change you."

"He won't." I met his eyes and smiled. "The second I met you, I knew he was wrong for me, so I think my filter's working okay."

Dash chuckled. "Any filter that keeps you with me is workin' just fine."

"You're a little biased, but I love that."

"And I love you, so it works out perfectly."

I grinned. "Back atya."

He kissed me, then started the shower. "You still good to hang at the bar tonight?"

"Yep. I'm kind of excited." I leaned against the bathroom counter. "I'm going to the taboo biker bar with my biker man and bucking the system."

Dash shook his head with a grin. "You're the original

rebel, baby."

"Next step, tattooing your name on my butt."

"You wanna tattoo my name on you, do it where people can see."

"I'm not sure I can do the neck. I hear it hurts."

He laughed. "Yeah, heard that too."

"Boob?"

"No touchin' the girls," he said. "Those are my fun bags and I don't want them marred."

I giggled. "Okay, fine. I'll do some more thinking."

"You do that." He kissed me. "You joinin' me?"

"Nope. I'm gonna go fix my man breakfast while he showers."

"Bacon."

"Of course, bacon. I'm not an animal."

He grinned, kissing me again. "You good?"

"Better than good, honey. Thank you."

"I won't be long."

I nodded and left him to shower, pulling on a pair of sweats, and heading downstairs to cook for my man.

* * *

Dash

I WALKED DOWNSTAIRS to the smell of bacon…and a man's voice, too low for me to tell who it was, so I sped up my pace a little, arriving in the kitchen to find Badger sitting at the island. "Hey, man."

"Hey," I said, pouring myself a cup of coffee. "You find somethin' out?"

"Yep. Figured you'd want to see it." He slid a manila folder toward me.

"What's that?" Willow asked.

"We think this is what the Torrance Group killed your father for."

"Who is the Torrance Group?"

Badger took a swig of coffee, then said, "From what we've been able to piece together from your father's files, they're a shell corporation made up of three local real estate investors. Your father kept a ledger containing entries of over forty real estate transactions in this, and the surrounding counties. The Torrance Group made every purchase and each one for a steal."

I nodded, skimming through the paperwork. "Your father encoded the names of those involved."

"He *was* kind of a code nut," Willow said. "He was obsessed with documentaries about cracking the Enigma code during the war and he'd always leave notes around the house with secret messages for me to figure out."

"What we don't know is if it was to protect them, or so he'd have leverage over them," I said.

"Neither sounds like my father. It's more likely that he was gathering information in order to confront them."

"It's obvious they were trying to get him to sell the church land. After he'd refused several offers, they must have started threatening him."

Willow hummed in thought. "Richard Waters was in my father's office and they were arguing about something."

"When?"

"A week or so before the shooting..." A look of realization flashed over Willow's face. "Wait a minute, let me see that ledger." I handed it to her and she counted something with her fingertip. "There are thirteen letters in Richard Waters' name."

"So?" I said.

"So, the name at the top of the third column has thirteen characters. I'll bet that's him."

Badger perked up. "We can use the letters in his name to crack the code!"

After a few minutes, we had all three names; Richard Waters, Judge Spencer Hayworth and most notably, Percy

Aljets, the deputy mayor of Savannah and father of Brad Aljets. Between the three of them, the members of the Torrance Group had ties in every possible facet of life in Savannah. It would have been relatively easy for them to intimidate, blackmail, pay off, or simply 'disappear' anyone they had to.

"Those bastards," Willow said softly, and she looked like she was forcing back tears. "They killed him just because he wouldn't give in to their greed."

"But he didn't die for nothing Willow. He was smart and he knew you'd find this and figure it all out."

"I didn't do all this, *you* did."

"We did it together Willow. We're all in this together…and we're gonna make these mother fuckers pay."

She nodded and I hugged her quickly. "Okay, who wants bacon?" she asked.

"Me," Badger and I answered in stereo.

* * *

Willow

DASH AND I arrived at the bar and found Badger and Gator in the back dueling over a game of pool. I took Dash's hand and squeezed, grinning up at him. I couldn't believe how excited I was to hang out with everyone…I missed these men when I didn't see them, which shocked me to no end.

"Baby girl!" Gator bellowed and I grinned (as I felt my face heat). "Get over here and hug the old man."

"I'll get us some drinks," Dash said, and I continued toward Gator while he went to the bar.

Gator pulled me in for a bear hug, lifting me off the ground and I laughed as he kissed my cheek. He set me down and Badger did the same thing, then let me go when Dash yelled, "Get your fuckin' hands off my woman!"

Badger grinned and gave him a chin lift before walking me to a table in the corner, and I climbed up onto a stool. It wasn't lost on me that they'd put me in a highly protected area, no one behind me and three bikers (more were coming) in front of me.

Dash returned with a light beer for me and pulled a chair next to mine, close enough for our bodies to touch. As was my habit, I leaned against him as I watched Gator and Badger battle it out.

Just as I took a second swig of beer, Doc walked toward us, a very pissed off looking Olivia in front of him. He virtually lifted her into a chair at our table, leaning close and warning, "Do not move."

"Tristan—"

"No, Liv. You fuckin' keep your ass parked on this chair 'til I sort this out."

Doc walked away and Olivia's face blotched red as she stared daggers at him. If she'd been in a cartoon, I could imagine steam coming out of her ears.

Dash leaned over to me and whispered, "Don't ask."

I frowned. "What?"

"It's their business."

I let out a dramatic huff and pushed off my seat, stepping over to Olivia. Dash tried to stop me, but I rolled my eyes. If Olivia was upset, she needed support.

"Are you okay?" I asked.

Olivia glared at something over my head, then focused on me, pasting a smile on her face. "I'm good, Willow. There's just a certain man who seems to think I'm his business and it's annoying as hell."

Doc set a drink on the table and raised an eyebrow. "Heard it all before, Liv. Don't give a fuck."

Dash tugged me back to him and pulled me between his legs. "None of our business."

I gripped his cut and frowned. "Sometimes girls need to know they're supported by other girls, because it doesn't happen very much, so how about you chill out there a little, cupcake?"

"Cupcake?"

"Definitely." I kissed him, smiling against his lips. "See? Sweet like a cupcake."

Dash laughed. "Never say that again. Ever."

"Cheesecake?"

"Fuck!" he hissed as he continued to laugh. "No."

"Twinkie?"

"Will—"

"Snowball...no...ah...mmmm, ding dong."

"Getting closer," he said.

"Well, that *is* my favorite thing to put in my mouth," I teased.

"You keep doin' this, and I'm gonna take you into the bathroom and fuck you," he warned.

I shivered, leaning closer. "Save that thought for later...when we're in one of my bathrooms, which are clean."

He chuckled, kissing me deeply. "I reserve the right to drag you into a corner should you keep turnin' me on."

"Okay, honey. I'll give you that." I grinned. "But now I really do have to use the bathroom."

"I'll walk you."

"I can go to the bathroom all by myself. I'm a big girl."

"I'll go with you," Olivia said.

Doc frowned. "Liv—"

"For the love of God, Tristan. I can go to the bathroom with Willow," Olivia said, sliding off her stool and grabbing her purse. "You have an unobstructed eyeline to the door. Calm the hell down, big man."

Olivia and I headed to the restroom and I was dying to ask her why Doc was so protective of her, but Dash's words kept playing in my head.

Olivia and I did our thing, then while we were washing our hands, she said, "I was kidnapped."

"I'm sorry?"

She pulled her lipstick out of her purse and ran it over her lips. "The reason Doc's being a pain in the ass."

"Oh, my gosh, Olivia. That must have been horrible."

"It was, but it's over and he refuses to let me forget."

"I'm sorry." I didn't know what else to say. I couldn't even begin to imagine what any of that would be like.

"It's no biggie. I just didn't want you to worry about me. Tristan has that covered in spades."

I smiled at her in the mirror, and followed her out of the bathroom, down the hallway, past the bar…and froze. Olivia didn't notice I wasn't right behind her until she looked back and frowned. But I couldn't move. I was stuck in total complete and utter terror.

After a few moments, which felt like hours, I felt Dash's hands at my neck and lifting my face as he called my name. "Baby…talk to me. Are you okay?"

I gripped his cut, but I couldn't speak.

"Let's get her outside," Doc said, and Dash wrapped an arm around my waist and half-carried, half-walked me out the back door into a gravel parking lot.

"Willow?" Dash stroked my cheek. "I'm here. What's wrong baby? Fuck, talk to me."

I focused on Dash as my wrist was lifted. "Her pulse is racing," Doc said.

"My jacket. Someone get my fucking jacket!" Dash demanded when I started to shake, and Olivia rushed back inside, returning with his leather jacket.

Dash placed it over my shoulders and I burrowed into the warmth and fell against Dash as though his leather protected me somehow. "The…the…man…"

"What man, baby?"

"The man…who…who shot Daddy. He's in there."

"What the fuck?" he snapped.

I shook my head. "I just heard…his voice. I…I…" I dropped my head to his chest and burst into tears.

"Take her home, Olivia."

"No," I argued. "No. I need to—"

"You don't need to do shit right now, Willow." Dash held me tighter.

"We might not have another chance to find this sonofabitch. You just tell me where you were in the bar when you heard his voice, and what he sounds like."

"I heard him when Olivia and I walked by the bar. He's somewhere towards the end, near the payphones," I said, fighting back my tears as a feeling of rage started to burn in the pit of my stomach. "He's in there, Dash. The one with the Appalachian twang and the lisp that I heard in my father's office. He's the one that shot my dad."

Dash held me and kissed my forehead, before turning to Olivia. "I'm gonna get Gator to follow you home."

"I came with you on your bike, Dash," I reminded him.

"Liv can drive my truck," Doc offered. "I'll ride back with Dash."

Olivia nodded.

"Have Gator meet me in front."

Dash gave him a chin lift, kissed me gently, then headed back into the bar.

"You got your piece?" Doc asked Olivia as we walked.

"Yes," she said.

"If someone other than Dash, me, or Badger want into the house, you shoot 'em. Ask questions later."

"I will," she said.

"Seriously—"

"Ohmigod, Tristan. I heard you," she snapped. "If Gator's with us, we'll be fine. Stop with this alpha male crap. *Please.*"

He chuckled. "You're cute."

As they argued, I noticed there was something there under the surface…almost as though Olivia 'doth protest too much.' Doc treated her with total respect and I could tell he cared about her…and weirdly enough, Olivia seemed just as taken with him, but she was obviously fighting her attraction. Doc didn't seem to care, though. I turned my back and tried to give them some semblance of privacy until Gator approached, and Doc released us into his care.

SIXTEEN

Dash

I HAD TO slow my breathing and come up with a plan. If I rolled into the bar as hot as I was right now, I'd probably drag the bastard out to the street and kill him with my bare hands, but that wasn't how our club operated, and the last thing they needed from me was to attract more heat. Besides, I knew my being in jail for murder would only leave Willow exposed and unprotected.

Doc walked back in and found me. "You good?"

I nodded. "Go on back to the pool tables and tell Badger to be ready for something to go down."

"What exactly should we be prepared for?"

I shrugged. "Not sure. First I've got to figure out who this psychopathic hillbilly is and what crew he's with."

"How do you know he's even with a crew?"

"Because Willow said she heard him at the bar, and if he's sitting at the bar he's with someone," I said. "He's either a club member or he's in tight with one."

Doc scanned the bar. "Yeah, but who?"

"I'm gonna go find out. You go talk to the guys but keep it quiet Doc. Remember this is Barney's."

Barney's was sacred ground for any and all bikers. It was a holy temple built back when motorcycles first captured the imaginations of outlaws and outsiders all over this country. All crews were welcome, and the rules were simple.

No business and no violence—ever.

Should a member or an associate of a club spill blood on Barney's property, that club would be banned for life. Not too long ago, a Savannah chapter member of the Spiders knifed a member of the Apex Predators. The Spiders were banned, which essentially ended any and all goodwill toward their club in the area.

We made our way back inside, and I headed for the bar. As I casually weaved through the crowd, I spotted the cuts of several Dogs, as well as Raptors, but not quite as many as I'd hoped. The long bar was lined with patches from Southern Devil's Sons and Apex Predators, both one-percenter clubs filled with members capable of killing for profit. It's about what I expected to see, but not what I'd hoped for.

"I'll take a Grolsch," I said, waving to Rusty. I was near the end of the bar where Willow said she'd heard the shooter's voice. I was also in a position to see Doc and the others by the pool tables. Doc saw me and gave me a slight nod. I was now swimming in very dangerous waters, but at least I knew my crew had eyes on me.

"You sure you're old enough to drink that?" A Southern Devil's Sons member with a long graying beard asked dryly.

I said nothing and handed the bartender a ten.

"Oh, lookie here boys, one of them fire pups wandered over to the bar. This little doggie must be thirsty, or maybe he just don't know where his place is," a whiney voice called out.

I took a slow pull from my beer and looked to my right. Seated at the bar was a man wearing an orange trucker's hat and an Apex Predators cut with what looked like a brand new "1%" patch. His thick twang was unmistakably Appalachian, and he was missing several teeth, making him sound like an evil cartoon snake. Greasy, dirty blond hair hung down, framing his gaunt face.

"Just here to drink and shoot some pool like everyone else," I said flatly, my eyes locked on him.

"Well, you boys sure as shit don't do anything else," he spat out.

I wanted to tear this fuckin' shit stain apart, but had to keep my cool. I wasn't even sure if this was the right guy, not to mention there was a second shooter at the church that we knew nothing about.

"Let me buy you a drink," I said, in an effort to get closer to him. I needed to figure out as much as I could about who he was and who he ran with.

"I only drink with bikers. *Real bikers*. Not you fuckin' pussy, candy-ass wannabes."

I could smell his rancid breath from where I stood.

"Alright, Virus, remember where you are," the bartender warned.

"I know where the fuck I am, godammit. It's this little pup right here that don't know where he's at," he said, now standing. "Besides, if his crew ain't gonna take care of business, like men out on the street, they sure as shit ain't gonna spill blood in here. Here or anywhere!" he said to a round of laughter.

"Everyone knows the Dogs of Fire are fuckin' boy scouts that never get their hands dirty. Candy-ass sonsabitches, every one of 'em."

"You'd better get back over to your pool game, son," the bartender said, motioning to Doc and the others.

"Yeah," I said, then adding, "I'll see you around," as I walked by Virus.

* * *

Willow

I BUSIED MYSELF in the kitchen, trying not to obsess over what could be happening to Dash and the rest of the guys at the bar. Gator was on the sofa, glued to SportsCenter, and Olivia was at my kitchen island sipping on her second glass of wine.

I couldn't understand how they were both so calm and I said as much as I mixed a batch of chocolate chip cookie dough.

"Why do you think I'm on my second…ah, no, third… glass of wine?" Olivia asked as she poured another.

"And why do you think I'm watchin'…the women's doubles world tennis championship finals?" Gator challenged. "Relax. If Dash needs anything, he'll let us know."

I sighed, scooping dough onto a cookie sheet. "What if that guy hurts him?"

"He's not gonna hurt him, baby girl," Gator said. "Dash knows what he's doin'. The asshole won't even know he's lookin' at him."

I bit my lip. "I wish I had your confidence."

Before anyone could respond, the alarm beeped, and Dash called out, "It's us."

I left my cookies and rushed to the foyer. "Did you get him?"

Dash shook his head. "Couldn't do it at Barney's, so we're watchin' him for the moment."

Doc smiled. "Don't worry, Willow, we got you."

Dash kissed me quickly.

"What's that smell?" Badger asked.

"Chocolate chip cookies," I said.

"You made cookies?" Doc asked, rubbing his hands together.

"Help yourself," I said, and Doc left me and Dash in the foyer.

"Do you know him?" I asked.

"The guy who killed your dad?"

"No, the mailman," I retorted in exasperation. "Yes, the man who killed my dad."

"No. But I will."

"Meaning?"

Dash kissed me again, wrapping his arms around my waist. "Meaning, I got you."

"What's the plan, Dash."

"Well, I'm gonna get a beer, then once everyone leaves, I'm gonna fuck my woman."

"Dash," I hissed.

"You know I'm not gonna tell you that, Willow."

I frowned. "Then we should call Lisa."

"Not gettin' the cops involved until we know more."

"But she can help."

He shook his head. "Not open for discussion, baby."

"Don't do anything that'll get yourself hurt or killed, okay?" I begged. "It's not worth it."

"Willow." He cocked his head. "Who are you talkin' to? I got this."

I rolled my eyes. "One time, Dash, just once, I wish you wouldn't be so flippant with your safety. I fully understand you're my big strong man, but even you can't stop a bullet, and if anything happened to you, I'd be lost. I love you, honey. More than life itself."

He sighed, stroking my cheek. "I hear you, baby. I promise I'll be careful. I always am, but I'm a little extra cautious now that I have you. Got someone to come home to now."

I leaned up and kissed him again. "That is the correct answer, handsome."

He chuckled, and patted my bottom. "I'm ready for cookies."

"Come on, then."

We walked back to the kitchen and I washed my hands so I could go back to scooping cookie dough onto sheets.

"Holy shit, baby girl," Gator said with a full mouth. "These are the best damn cookies I've ever had."

I smiled. "It's Nestle, so I can't really take any credit for it."

"You know what would make 'em better?" he said.

"Enlighten me, old man."

"Pot."

"Holy shit, yes," Badger agreed. "Weed cookies would be fuckin' amazin'."

"It's legal in Portland," Doc said.

"So, we need a reason to visit the chapter out there, then," Gator said.

I shook my head. "You people are insane."

"You've obviously never had it," Badger teased. "Or you wouldn't say that."

"I only started drinking wine a year ago," I admitted. "It was frowned upon in my house, so, no I've never tried it."

"I don't like it," Olivia said. "It makes me paranoid."

Doc wrapped an arm around her waist. "You could always try it with me. I'll make sure you're not paranoid."

"Keep dreaming," she said, and took a bite of cookie.

"You got more beer?" Badger asked with his head in the fridge.

"No," Dash said. "Wasn't expectin' company."

"You really should have a couple cases in the garage just in case," Gator said.

"Should I?" Dash challenged.

"And a few bottles of wine," Olivia said.

I giggled. "We'll obviously need to plan better for the future."

"That'd be appreciated," Gator said.

"I think I need to plan to buy more food as well," I said, nodding toward Badger who was currently double-fisting cookies, while one was in his mouth.

"Does that mean you'll cook more?" Gator asked, hopefully.

I grinned. "You want me to cook more?"

"Yeah. I'll eat anything you cook. Never tasted better."

"Aw." I leaned over and kissed his cheek. "You're the sweetest man on the planet."

"Shit, baby girl. Don't tell no one that."

"My lips are sealed."

The rest of the night was spent hanging with everyone, and after Dash and Doc made a food and booze run, I forced them all into a game of charades, which got dirtier and dirtier the more alcohol was consumed.

I'd never had more fun in my life. Despite the fact my life was in chaos, I'd never felt calmer than when I was with Dash, and even though I was in danger, I'd never felt safer than with him and the Dogs.

All my life I'd been around sinners dressed up as saints, and here I was being accepted, loved, and protected by the very "undesirables" the town had warned me about all my life. Even my father, who loved everyone, was completely wrong about the Dogs of Fire. These people may be sinners in the eyes of the church, but they were saints to me, and more importantly they were becoming my family.

SEVENTEEN

Dash

I'D BARELY SLEPT the night before. Willow, on the other hand, was out the minute her head hit the pillow. I'm sure the wine helped, but there was something more. She seemed happier than I'd ever seen her. There was a light in her eyes last night that I wanted to see every day. I, however, was awake all night thinking about how to protect the woman I love, and how I was going to make the people that killed her father pay.

My phone rang and I answered before it woke Willow. I'd tasked Badger with tailing Virus last night and had been waiting for his call.

"Hey, man. Whatcha got?"

"I followed him to a place out in the woods near Sugar Falls Creek. He's holed up in a cabin with four or five other guys. I see three bikes parked out front and two trucks. They've got a couple of pallets of supplies and a guard posted on the front porch. It looks like a private party, and it looks like they're fixin' to be here a while."

"Sounds like we just might need to crash that party."

"I'm in," he said.

"All right, text me the location and sit tight. I'll be there as soon as I can." I hung up and carefully slid out of bed. Willow stirred and I bent down and kissed her forehead. "Go back to sleep, baby, I just need to go check on something. I'll be back before you know it."

"What?" she grumbled. "Where are you going? What time is it?"

"It's just past six a.m., go back to sleep. Gator'll be here when you wake up."

She muttered something incoherent and immediately began snoring again. Even when passed out she was fucking adorable.

I got dressed and hit the road. I loved riding in the early hours of the morning, especially on days like this, when there was hardly anyone else out. The past month or so had been a blur, and it was only during moments like this, riding alone, with only the sound of my V-twin motor to drown out the noise of the world, that I could clearly hear my own thoughts. It had been this way for me since the first time I got on a motorcycle.

It's why I still rode, and why I belonged to the Dogs of Fire crew. Our club believed that in order to ride free, you have to truly be free. That was what guys like Virus and those shitty biker thugs would never understand. They loved money, power, and violence, and there was no freedom to be found in those things. That kind of life leads to a jail cell or a pine box, and you can't ride when you're inside either of those.

The sun was just starting to peek over the horizon when I reached the small road that led to the cabin. I checked my GPS and killed the engine. I rolled my bike to the thick brush where Badger told me he'd stashed his, and quietly made my way down the road where he was waiting.

"Dash, over here," I heard him whisper. "Over here, man." I followed his voice and found him hidden behind a small group of trees, with a clear view of the cabin.

"What's the story?" I asked.

"The main road over there leads to the house. It's the only way in or out and they've got a chain up."

"What about personnel?"

"Well, that big fucker there with the shotgun has been on the front porch all night, and the rest of the crew is inside with Virus."

"You're still thinking there are five or six guys in there?" I asked. He'd texted me a few details earlier which was why I was coming in silently so to speak.

"As far as I could see when they pulled in last night. I had a pretty good tail on Virus when he left Barney's around two in the morning. By the time I had snuck up to the cabin he was going at it pretty good with his crew. I couldn't make out what they were fighting about, but they sounded pretty pissed."

"Okay, thanks Badger, I'm gonna try to get close to the house to see if I can get a better headcount. Hang back here, but be ready in case anything jumps off."

Cutting through the woods as quietly as possible, I made my way around the back of the cabin. I couldn't see a guard posted at the rear, but proceeded with caution as I made my way closer. I could smell coffee brewing and could hear the sounds of heavy boots on the cabin's hardwood floor as I approached. I crouched below an open window, careful to stay out of sight. The only thing we had going for us was the element of surprise.

"Wake the fuck up! It's your turn to get the firewood," I heard a voice bellow from inside.

"What the hell, motherfucker! I was asleep, you prick," Virusd whined in protest.

"Well, you ain't asleep now, so get up and go get some firewood from the shed."

"Okay, keep it down, Bull, I'm hung over as hell."

"No shit, asshole! That's because you snuck out and got hammered last night."

"Not this shit all over again. It ain't a big deal. I told you last night, it was just me and a bunch of our crew…and some Devil's Sons. It's Barneys man, nobody's gonna fuck with me there. It's safe."

"Safe, my ass, and that ain't the point! Prez told you stay low for a while and he told me to keep eyes on you at all times. If he knew you were out on the fuckin' town last night, it'd be both our asses, not to mention what Mr. Aljets would do."

"Two things, brother. First, I don't answer to that Aljets prick, and second, he didn't see me last night."

"You'd better hope no one else did either."

"I told you, the place was filled with friendly faces. It was all Predators and Sons…except for a few Raptors and a handful of those Dogs pussies."

"There were Dogs there?"

I heard Bull's tone change sharply.

"Which Dogs?" A third voice asked.

"I dunno. I saw that Gator prick there, and a couple other guys. Some pretty boy dickhead too."

"Pretty boy? Are you talking about Dash?" Bull asked slowly.

"I dunno. That could have been his name. He came up to the bar and was acting like a badass. Fuck him and fuck the Dogs of Fire."

"You fucking redneck idiot! The Dogs of Fire were the first ones to arrive at the church after you and Tucker shot the place to hell. Dash and his crew have already been questioned by the cops and are now apparently poking around."

"So the fuck what?"

"If Dash and the Dogs have sniffed you out, Mr. Aljets will find out, and take care of you himself."

"I ain't afraid of him and I ain't afraid of some chicken shit club! Aljets hired us to kill them church people and make it look like some random shoot up and that's what we did. It ain't my fault the Dogs showed up, and it ain't my fault that killing the old man didn't solve all of Aljet's problems."

"What about that dead little girl, you piece of shit? Whose fault was that?"

"C'mon man, this again? I already told you that was an accident. Me and Tucker fired off a few rounds and one of 'em went through the wall and hit that little girl."

I heard Bull spit at Virus. "You're a piece of shit, and patch or no patch, you're gonna fucking answer for this someday."

"We was just doin' what the prez and that Aljets fucker said to do. Make it look random!"

"Then why shoot the preacher five times? Don't you think that makes him look like the intended target?"

"I dunno, I just hated that smug old bastard. Why wouldn't he just sell that old church? He was standing in the way of the club makin' a lot of money, Bull, and I'm sick of running small time jobs. This thing with Aljets and them Torrance guys is big time, and the club stands to make more money than we ever seen. That stubborn fucker got what was coming and I'd do it again."

I could barely hear what Bull said next. The loud pulse of blood rushing to my head drowning out the sounds around me. My blood boiled and I had to focus on staying perfectly still to keep myself from leaping through the open window and choking Virus to death.

"Just go get the firewood and I'll go wake up fuckup number two," Bull said. "The Prez and the VP are coming by and I sure as shit ain't making breakfast."

I quietly sprung for the tree line before Virus made his way out the back door. I could spy him through the trees, heading for a small woodshed, near where their bikes were parked. I also spotted something else about twenty yards away from the house that gave me an idea. I made my way back to Badger and clued him in on the plan.

"Okay, I need you to go hide out by the chain that's blocking the road. With any luck, in a few minutes Virus is goin' to come haulin' ass down the road and will need to drop the chain to get out. When he does, lay low and be ready."

"Ready for what?" Badger asked.

"To lock up behind him after he leaves." I smiled and patted him on the back before heading for my bike.

I quietly rolled it as far down the road as I could before reaching the chain. I could just make out Badger's burly frame hidden in the leaves and brush, and gave him a nod before positioning myself. I straddled my bike and drew my pistol. There was enough light to see Virus gathering wood from the shed and my intended target; a five-hundred-gallon propane tank.

I fired off three rounds in quick succession before penetrating the tank which erupted in a glorious ball of flame. The windows of the cabin were instantly blown out and the shockwave of the massive blast sent Virus to his ass, firewood toppling on him as he fell. However, he didn't stay down for long, which is exactly what I was counting on. He scrambled to his feet, and I fired up my bike, revving the throttle in order to get his attention. He spotted me and did exactly as I'd hoped, and went straight for his bike, which was parked just by the shed. He raced toward me as I took off for the highway. He stopped, unhooked the chain gate and continued his pursuit. Badger's job was to hang the chain back up as soon as Virus was out of sight, in order to delay the rest of his crew.

I flew down the road at top speed. I knew Virus would be armed; hell, I was *counting* on it, and I also figured his bike would be fast, so my head start was crucial. What Badger, or any of my other club members didn't know was that I had an ace hidden up my sleeve. Well, technically she was hidden behind the Shake Shack where the highway meets Old Mill road. I voice activated my blue tooth and when she answered, yelled, "We're almost there! Get Ready!"

"Roger."

Clank! The sound of a bullet hitting my exhaust pipe nearly toppled me, so I leaned down a bit. I was already fully gunning my bike and keeping ahead of Virus pretty good, but bullets are faster than Harleys, and another whizzed by my head as I rode on. I took the next exit and floored it around the tight curve, leaning in as low as I could. As I turned onto Old Mill road, I felt the impact of what felt like a baseball bat to my left shoulder, and I almost lost control of my bike. I looked down to see the upper sleeve of my jacket torn and blackened. For a few moments I felt nothing, followed by an intense searing heat, as if being branded.

Fuck, I'm shot.

Doing my best to ignore the pain, I pushed my bike into the red again and sped through the final fifty yards of our chase. I headed for the Shake Shack with Virus right on my tail, gun still drawn and haulin' ass.

As we rounded the corner, Lisa and her partner, who had been waiting in an unmarked car, pulled up behind Virus, and hit the lights and sirens. As soon as they did, four additional squad cars appeared from their hiding spot around the back, forcing Virus to pull over.

I parked my bike which was now leaking more fluid than I was, and sat my ass on the gravel. I wasn't sure if I was more pissed off that he shot me or my bike. Either way, this asshole was going to pay...for everything. Assessing my current state of health, I pushed myself up and headed for Virus, ready to take him down a few pegs. Before I could reach him, however, the cops had Virus hogtied and Lisa was reading him his rights.

I bent down to address Virus, his greasy face still pressed against the asphalt. "You're gonna pay for every life you took, and I'm going to personally make sure you pay extra for the little girl and for Willow's father."

"Are you hearing this?" Virus snapped. "He's threatenin' me."

"I'm sorry?" Lisa countered, pressing her foot into his back. "What was that?"

"Nice try, asshole," I hissed.

"Fuck you, pretty boy," was all Virus could manage. "You got nothin'."

"Except for your .38, which is the same caliber as the weapon used in Mr. Miller's shooting," Lisa said. "I'm gonna bet you were stupid enough to keep the gun you used, and that this is it."

Virus's normal yellow complexion turned white.

"Not to mention, the pile of weapons and drugs we found back at your safe house," Lisa continued. "That's right. We've got half your club locked up right now, and I'd bet they're already turning on you."

"Fuck you, pig bitch."

I leaned in closer. "You're gonna burn, your club is gonna burn, and then we're coming after Torrance."

Virus's eyes widened. "I d...don't...know...what...what you're talking about."

"I think you do. I also think you're gonna have a hell of a time avoiding being shanked in county lockup. The only question is, will Aljets pay someone in your club do it, or will they volunteer?"

Two officers picked Virus up and stuffed him in the

back of a squad car.

"Thanks, Lisa," I said.

She nodded. "This is going to be a paperwork nightmare, and I'm going to have to leave a couple minor details out of my report, but we got him."

"Minor details, huh? Like that propane tank back at the safe house?"

"You mean the leak that caused the explosion?" she asked, smiling. "Catching him speeding through town, guns blazing, will be enough for us to keep him in custody as long as we need to smooth everything over—" She paused, suddenly noticing my arm. "Have you been shot?"

"Yeah, but I'll have Doc take care of it."

"Like hell you will, we have to get you to a hospital."

"It's not a big deal, the bullet grazed me."

"Not a big deal? You're shot and you're bleeding Dash."

"I'll be okay. Besides, I think the less of a paper trail there is regarding today's events, the better. Don't you? Trust me, there's no one better in the field than Doc. I could use a lift, though, my bike was hit too."

"No problem," Lisa said. "We'll get someone to haul your bike back to your compound, too."

"Appreciate that."

I climbed into Lisa's cruiser and once she'd finished at the scene, she drove me back to the compound.

EIGHTEEN

Willow

I WAS IN the kitchen making Gator lunch, when he let out the worst string of swear words on the planet and jumped off the sofa.

"What's wrong?" I asked.

"That fuckin', wet behind the ears, fuckin'—"

"Gator!" I snapped.

He glanced at me and scowled. "Give me a second, Willow. Got a situation."

He put his phone to his ear and walked toward the slider, but I heard "Dash," so I followed.

"Why the fuck didn't he tell anyone?" Gator snapped as he stepped onto the deck. "Yeah? Oh, really? That fuckin'... no, fuck! Is he dead?"

My heart stopped and I grabbed his arm. "What is going *on*?"

"Yeah, she's here. Where the hell else would she be?"

I bit back tears as I squeezed his arm. I wanted to puke, but I needed to know what was wrong first.

"No, Doc, this is bullshit. Yeah, I can fuckin' bring her, but I reserve the right to beat the shit out of that kid first." He nodded. "No, goddammit, that little shit's got some explainin' to do." He met my eyes and his face softened. "Yeah, we're leavin' now."

He hung up and guided me back into the house. "Grab your purse, babe, we need to get to the compound."

"What's going on?"

"Dash has had a little accident."

I gasped, rushing for the closet. "What kind of accident?"

"Nothin' major, baby girl. He's all good. Just needs a few stitches."

"Stitches?" I squeaked. "What happened?"

"He got shot."

"What?" I rasped, bursting into tears. "Is he okay? Is he dead?"

"Did ya miss the part where I said he was all good?" Gator deadpanned.

"Snarky is not the way to go here, old man," I ground out, scooping my keys off the foyer console.

"He's fine, baby girl. Flesh wound. Doc's sewin' him up at the compound." He snatched the keys from my hand and said, "I'm drivin'."

"I'm not riding with you," I countered. I was fine to get on the back of Dash's bike, but the thought of getting on anyone else's was just too much. Especially in my current state of vulnerability.

"I'm gonna drive your car," he clarified. "Come on."

I followed Gator out of the house and after he locked

up, we headed to the compound. He had to pull over a couple of times because I was sick to my stomach, but we made it in less time than normal because Gator drove like a maniac.

Gator led me back to Doc's clinic and I walked in to see bloody rags on the floor and Dash on his back, one leg bent at the knee, his face turned to the wall, while Doc stitched his arm.

"Oh!" I whispered, the sight of my man injured overwhelming.

Dash's head whipped to me and he scowled. "Get her out of here!"

"Are you okay?"

"I'm fine, baby, but you need to wait outside." He hissed out an expletive when Doc dug the needle back into his arm.

"Why isn't he at a hospital?" I demanded.

"Gator! Fuck!" Dash snapped. "Get her out!"

Gator wrapped an arm around my waist and tugged, but I wouldn't budge.

"You're hurt and in pain and you think I'm leaving you?" I asked, sobbing.

Dash sat up slightly. "Goddammit! Gator!"

Gator dragged me out of the room and even though I dug my heels in, I was no match for the much larger man.

He released me once we were in the hallway, but refused to let me back in the room…and believe me, I tried. I even resorted to physical violence, but Gator just grabbed my arms gently and held them away from his body with a chuckle.

"You can go in when Dash says it's okay to go in…but after I beat the shit out of him, got it?"

"If you touch him, I will maim you."

"Yeah, I can see you have that power, baby girl," he deadpanned.

Before I could eviscerate him with my words…my

clean words since swearing still wasn't something I could bring myself to do...Doc pulled the door open and gave the all-clear.

I pushed away from Gator and rushed into the room. Dash was sitting on the edge of the exam bed, his arm bandaged, and even though he looked wrecked, he held his arm out to me and I closed the distance between us.

"What happened?" I asked, as he pulled me between his legs.

"Long story, baby, can I fill you in when I'm not feelin' so out of it?"

"How about you give me the short version to tide me over?"

He sighed. "Followed the guy who shot your dad, found him and a few of his friends, chase and gunfire ensued, I got clipped, the bad guys got nabbed."

"Gunfire?" I snapped. "As in raining bullets kind of gunfire?"

"Baby, seriously, I'm good."

"Give us a minute, baby girl," Gator said.

"No."

"Willow," he growled.

"No. Whatever you have to say to him, you can say in front of me. I'm not leaving him."

"I need to crash," Dash said. "Want me to crash here or at your place?"

"Are you seriously asking me that right now?"

"Tryin' to be sensitive, Willow."

"Why start now?" I retorted. "My place. Come on."

After getting instructions from Doc on how to care for the wound and what to watch for, he gave me a prescription for painkillers, and Gator helped Dash to the car. Dash had been shot in almost the exact place I had been, so I was fairly confident I'd have no issues taking care of him, and bonus, according to Dash, we'd have matching scars. It's weird what guys think about.

Gator refused to leave even though Dash fell asleep on the sofa. I didn't mind, I liked having Gator around, but I had a feeling he was hanging around in order to yell at my man and I wasn't a big fan of that fact, and I told him as much. Unfortunately, his "grievances" fell under Club business, therefore, they were none of mine.

"Are you staying for dinner?" I asked Gator while he flipped through the channels on the TV.

"Does a bear shit in the woods?"

"Since they live there, most definitely."

"What are you making?"

"Does it matter?" I challenged. "I could hand you a poop sandwich and you'd probably eat it."

"Poop sandwich. Fuck me, baby girl, you're a hoot." He roared with laughter, startling Dash who sat up like someone had just slapped him, and his eyes found mine.

"You okay?" he asked.

"I'm good, honey," I said, and rushed to him. "Can I get you anything?"

"No, I'm okay."

Gator's laughter stopped, his face taking on a rather glary scowl, and I frowned. "I'm going to get the casserole in the oven. You be nice."

I waited until he nodded before kissing Dash gently, then walking back to the kitchen. I watched them closely as they spoke in whispers, looking for any sign that Gator might 'beat the shit' out of Dash, but they appeared to be playing nice for the moment, so I focused on the food.

"You goddamn, little shit!" Gator bellowed, and I nearly dropped the pan I was holding.

"Gat—"

"No, boy, you listen to me." He rose to his feet and jabbed a finger at him. "You went in there without backup. Forget the fact you didn't call me, I'm more pissed you didn't let the rest of the brothers in on the plan. One for backup wasn't a good choice."

"Badger was enough, brother. Plus, we had Lisa. You had to be here with Willow," Dash countered.

"And I'm fuckin' fine with that. I wouldn't be a good backup choice anyway, but you shoulda told me."

I could tell Gator was hurt because he hadn't been kept in the loop, and I was grateful he was using his words, but I could also tell Dash wasn't getting the nuances of why Gator was upset.

"Gator, buddy, do you want cheese on this?"

My question distracted him enough to get his focus off of Dash, and he sauntered into the kitchen and sat at the island. "Whatya thinkin'?"

"I'm making a chicken, bacon, and cheese pasta casserole, but would you prefer cheddar or mozzarella on the top?"

"How about both?"

I smiled. "I can do that."

"I'm gonna take a walk. Be back in a bit," he said, and left the house.

After cheesing the casserole, I made my way to the sofa and sat beside Dash who dragged a hand over his face. "He's pretty pissed, huh?"

I nodded. "But I don't think you're fully understanding why he's so upset."

"Yeah?"

"He was worried, Dash. He loves you like a son, and me like a daughter, and regardless of the fact we have no blood ties, we're his family. He's already gone through the biggest loss a person can endure, so you nearly getting killed was probably a trigger." I laid my hand on his thigh. "He didn't really care about backup…at least, I don't think he did. He trusts you, but if you'd let him in on the plan, he would have at least felt a little needed. You know what I mean?"

"Yeah, baby, I know what you mean." Dash sighed. "Why the hell do I feel like I just disappointed my dad?"

"Because you kind of did." I leaned over and kissed him. "But he'll get over it...once you apologize."

"You're makin' me soft."

I smiled. "That's not what you said last night."

"So very true." Dash chuckled. "Love you, baby."

"I love you, too. Now, do you want some painkillers? You're due."

He nodded. "Yeah, that'd be good."

Gator walked back in just as Dash took his pill, so Dash ushered him outside so they could 'talk.' I gave them their space and finished up dinner, greatly relieved when my men walked back in and the smile was back on Gator's face.

"The casserole's in the oven," I said. "So, do you want chocolate cake or chocolate chip cookies for dessert?"

"Both," Dash and Gator said, simultaneously.

I chuckled. "Alrighty, then, you're going to have to help."

Gator didn't hesitate, walking to the sink to wash his hands while Dash pulled me in for another kiss. "You're a genius, you know that, right?"

I grinned. "Sure do."

* * *

AS I BRUSHED my teeth and got ready for bed, Dash filled me in on the day's events and I forced myself not to panic as he gave me a detailed blow-by-blow.

"Lisa's sure the charges will stick?"

"Well, she's a cop, not a DA, but she says the arrest was solid, so she's confident. The guy *was* speeding through town shooting a .38 pistol after all. Besides, the main goal here is to make him sweat as much as possible so he'll give us information on Torrance."

Dash sat against the headboard of the bed, shirtless and delicious, and it took everything I had not to jump on him.

"Let me check your bandage," I said, sitting beside

him, and reaching for the wrap.

"Feel like getting out of here for a few days?"

I wiped the blood gently from his arm, placed a fresh square of gauze over the wound, then wrapped it back up. "Are you worried?"

"Just want to get you out of here 'til the heat dies down. We could take a road trip to Brooke's, make a weekend of it."

"I don't have anything on my plate until Wednesday, so I think that sounds fun."

"Bike's shot to hell, so we'll have to take your car…"

I grimaced. "There's no way I'd want to take your bike, anyway. I like to listen to music and sleep on long road trips, so being on the back of your Harley would not work for me. I'll let you drive, though."

"Oh, yeah?"

"Yeah." I grinned. He hated being locked in a "cage." Dash wasn't a fan of driving, period, so I typically drove when we had to take my car for anything.

"Well, thanks, baby. You're so selfless…and giving… and shit."

"Call it penance for putting yourself in a dangerous situation and getting *shot*."

He sighed. "Willow."

"What were you thinking?" I snapped. "You could have been killed!"

All of my pent-up fears and frustrations came pouring out as I finally let the day's events register in my heart and mind. Dash pulled me onto his lap and stroked my back as I raged against him.

"What if you were killed, Dash? What if I lost you, too?" I sobbed. "I couldn't bear it. You're a jerk for almost taking yourself away from me."

"I know, baby. I'm sorry."

"See? I don't actually believe you *are* sorry. You can only be sorry if you regret what you did and never intend on doing it again, and I just don't think you do. I think you feel absolutely justified in your actions."

"You're right, Willow, I do."

"Exactly. Which means, it doesn't really matter what my thoughts and feelings are on the subject, because the end justifies the means."

He sighed. "I hear you."

"*Do* you hear me, Dash?" I ground out. "Do you? Because if you ever do this again, I'll be done."

He shook his head. "Huh-uh, we're not playin' that game."

"This isn't a *game!*" I pushed off his lap and waved my hands in the air in frustration. "You were almost *killed*, Dash. Dead…forever. Gone. I can't do this if every time you walk out that door, I won't be sure you're coming back to me."

"Baby, I could walk out that door and get hit by a bus, nothing in this life is guaranteed."

"But you don't need to walk out the door and step directly in front of it! It's almost like you don't care…like you have a death wish and the rest of us who love you be damned."

"Goddammit, Willow, that's not fair."

"It's not fair that you put yourself in the path of a bullet, but I'm supposed to stand here like the dutiful girlfriend and accept it? No. I won't do it." I left him on the bed, rushing downstairs and out onto the deck. I needed the fresh air…desperate for the feeling of being drowned to go away.

I hadn't been outside for long when Dash joined me, leaning against the railing with his arms crossed, watching me.

"What?" I asked.

"I'm an ass."

"Tell me something I don't know."

He sighed, reaching a hand out to me. I hesitated for a

brief second before walking into his arms. "I'm sorry, baby."

I nodded against his chest. "*And?*"

"And I won't do it again. I promise."

"Because..."

He lifted my head and smiled. "Because now I have more to lose, and the thought of you sad makes me crazy."

"Next time you'll leave this kind of thing to the police, right?"

"Yeah, baby, I'll leave it all to the cops next time."

I sagged against him. "Are you just saying that because I'm upset, or do you really understand where I'm coming from?"

"I get it." He kissed the top of my head. "Fuck, baby, I didn't think, you're right. I'm not used to people givin' a shit, but you and Gator kinda shone some light on that today. The last thing I want you to do is worry about me...especially, if it's because I'm doin' somethin' reckless."

I leaned back to meet his eyes. "So, you admit it was reckless, then."

"Yeah, baby, I admit it. Keep beatin' the fuckin' dead horse, though, and I might get a little pissed."

I frowned. "I'm gonna let that snarky comment go, because I like that you're hearing me and I'm relieved you're not dead. But for future reference, telling me not to beat a dead horse, when that horse is you being a jerk, won't go well for you."

He grinned. "I'm glad I'm not dead, too, baby. And I'll keep your warning in mind, but right now, you're fuckin' sexy as hell all bossy and shit, and I kinda want to fuck you senseless."

"Dash," I admonished. "You were just shot this morning."

"Not in the dick."

"This is true, but I don't want you pulling those stitches."

He kissed me gently. "You let me worry about pullin' the stitches, yeah? You just need to decide whether you want be fucked over the sofa or in bed."

"What about both?" I rasped.

"Correct answer."

He guided me back inside, locked up again and proceeded to 'fuck me senseless.'

NINETEEN

Willow

DASH GUIDED THE car into the driveway of a large, newer brick home in Atlanta. As we'd driven through the neighborhood, we'd passed a large community pool, tennis and basketball courts, and I was impressed with how neat and tidy everyone's lawns were. It was the quintessential American neighborhood and I loved it.

Before we could get out of the car, a beautiful woman rushed out the front door and let out a loud, "Squee! You're here!"

Dash chuckled, climbing out of the car and catching her as she threw herself into his arms. I felt a little like I was crashing their emotional reunion, so I popped the trunk and reached in to grab one of the bags.

"Baby, what the hell are you doin'?" Dash said, pulling my hand away from the duffel and tugging me toward his aunt. "I'll get those. Come and meet Brooke."

I took a deep (silent) breath and followed him out from behind the car. Brooke grinned, wrapping her arms around me and hugging me tight.

"Ohmigod, girl, you are stunning." She leaned away, cupping my face. "When Finn said he was bringing home a girl to meet me...the first one, ever, I might add...I had no idea she'd be as gorgeous as you."

Brooke had deep blue eyes, and looked more like Dash than I expected...she really could be his mom...which made me even more curious to know about his family.

"Hey, now," Dash piped in.

"What?" she challenged, wrapping an arm around my shoulders. "You need to learn something, baby boy. When your kid tells you he's joinin' a motorcycle club and your favorite show is Sons of Anarchy, you get a little nervous about what said kid has gotten himself into. I was expecting a biker ho, but you brought me an angel, I'm not complaining."

"Not one—"

"Percenters, yeah, I know, kid," she retorted. "Doesn't mean I'm not gonna worry." I smiled, immediately at ease, and let her lead me into the house. "Tony's keeping the boys occupied so you're not bombarded with nosy questions."

"I don't mind," I said. "I love kids."

The second those words left my lips, two dark-headed boys came running toward us as though they'd just escaped some form of prison.

"Where's Finn?" the eldest demanded.

I knew Jase was ten and Evan was seven, but outside

of that, I didn't know a whole bunch about Dash's cousins. Looking at them now, however, I knew they'd grow up to be total heartbreakers.

Brooke tussled his hair and said, "He's coming, Jase, but how about you meet Willow first? I did teach you manners, right?"

He grinned, sticking his hand out to me. "I'm Jase Allen, it's nice to meet you, Willow."

I shook his hand. "Nice to meet you, too."

"And I'm Evan," the little one said, mimicking his brother.

"It's lovely to meet both of you."

"Dudes! Where are my helpers?" Dash bellowed. "I can't carry all this crap by myself, I need some brothers to help me."

The boys didn't hesitate to run to assist and I didn't miss the fact he censored his potty mouth…apparently, Dash *was* teachable.

A tall man, probably early fifties (I had to guess because Dash knew nothing about birthdays and ages outside of his aunt's), walked toward us and smiled. He was also completely bald, so it was always hard for me to gauge someone's age without hair.

"Hey. I'm Tony."

I grinned, shaking his hand. "Willow."

"Just leave the bags, Finn," Tony said. "Come eat. I'm grillin'."

Dash dropped our luggage with a huge grin and nodded. "Did you use your marinade?"

"Did I use my marinade?" Tony scoffed. "Of course I used my marinade, I'm not an animal."

Dash scooped Evan onto his shoulders and asked, "Who wants Dad's steaks?"

"Me!" Evan bellowed, waving his hands in the air.

Jase grinned and walked backwards, while he peppered Dash with a million questions. "Can we throw the football around?"

"Yeah, buddy, of course."

"Can we play Call of Duty later?"

"That's up to Mom. But I'll put in a good word." Dash kept Evan secure as he followed Jase out to the back, winking at me as he passed.

Brooke looped her arm in mine and gave me a gentle squeeze. "God damn, I love that boy."

I sighed. "Me too."

"I can tell." She smiled through watery eyes. "I'm really glad you're here, honey. It was him and me against the world for the longest time before Tony, and if we hadn't had to move here for his job, I would have insisted we stay wherever Finn was. I begged him to come with us, but he wouldn't have any of it."

"That's because he's his own man. Obviously because you raised him to be."

"Yeah, I guess that's true."

"You raised a really great man, Brooke. He's humble and he knows how to make me feel loved and cherished. He's almost perfect, if you ask me, and that's because of you. He might not say it enough, but he loves you to pieces, and he misses you terribly...and his brothers. He never takes for granted the sacrifices you made for him and neither will I. Thank you for him. I praise God everyday he came into my life, and I'll make sure we visit more often."

Brooke burst into tears and pulled me in for a long hug. "Holy, shit, girl, I really didn't want to cry so soon in our visit."

I chuckled through watery tears of my own. "Well, I think it's important we tell each other how much we mean to one another, but I have a feeling Dash hasn't always done that with you, but he tells me how he feels about you, so I'm relaying the message."

"Mom? You okay?" Dash asked, walking back in the door.

"I'm good, honey," she said, but cried even harder as he wrapped his arms around her and pulled her close.

This was the first time I'd heard him call her 'Mom.' He usually referred to her as his aunt or Brooke, and I never questioned it, since it was technically true. But standing before us now was a young man worried about the woman who'd mothered him when he didn't have one, and I found myself wiping away tears that streamed down my face.

"Holy shit, what the fuck happened?" he asked, reaching out for me.

We ended up in a three-way hug, with me and Brooke crying all over his shirt.

"Language, Finn," she warned, and he laughed.

"Hey Pot, I'm Kettle."

She giggled, squeezing him tight. "I love you."

"Love you, too," he said.

"I'm going to wash my face real quick and then we'll get our eat on."

She walked away and Dash met my eyes. "What happened?"

"I just told her what an amazing man she'd raised and how much I appreciated her."

He chuckled, kissing me gently. "I love you, baby."

"Love you more."

He held me for a few precious moments so that I could 'cry it out,' then he kissed me again and we headed outside to where the boys were tossing a football around. Dash joined his brothers when Brooke returned with a bottle of wine and some glasses.

We stayed outside until the moon had almost completely risen, and as I sat curled up in an overstuffed chair with Dash, a sense of peace I'd never felt before washed over me. He was my center, he was my calm, and in so many ways, he'd saved me.

The biker and the preacher's daughter...two people

destined to never cross paths...but two people who needed each other, and fit better than fate or God or whatever could have designed.

I kissed him gently and then snuggled closer as he joked around with his family. This was exactly where I was supposed to be.

EPILOGUE

Willow

Two years later…

WELL, I WAS officially a teacher. Today was my first day at my new career and I was nervous. Dash had cleared his schedule so he could drive me, but he was dilly-dallying with coffee or something…I didn't know because I was blinded by panic as I rushed downstairs looking for my jacket.

"Babe!"

"What?" I called out as I opened the closet.

"If you're looking for your jacket, it's in here…where you left it last night…so you wouldn't be late."

I wrinkled my nose in frustration. "Oh, right."

I headed into the kitchen and Dash chuckled. "Baby, you've got an hour before you even have to be there."

"*No*," I countered. "I have an hour before class starts…I need to be there in twenty-seven minutes."

He wrapped his arms around me and held me tight.

"Dash, I need to go."

He kissed my nose. "Actually, you need to chill for a second."

I huffed, leaning against him.

"Have I told you how cute you are when you're in a panic?" he asked.

"No, because it's not true. Didn't count on this when you put a ring on it, huh?"

He laughed. "I sure as fuck did. I bought the cow and everything that came along with her…especially those glorious udders." He cupped my breasts and squeezed gently.

We'd been married for about eighteen months now, and we loved every second of it. We'd had a little hiccup at the beginning when Dash slipped a prenup in front of me and forced me to sign. He wanted nothing to do with my money, and had Levi draw up the documents making sure my inheritance was protected should we divorce.

My whole argument had been that there would never be a divorce, just his dead body Jasmine and Parker would have to help me hide, so a prenup was unnecessary. In the end, I did sign it, but only because he refused to marry me if I didn't. I figured he couldn't stop me from spending the money on him if I so chose, so it was really a moot point.

I'd never thought being joined to someone forever would be so darn fun, especially, since the little issue of my life being threatened was dealt with.

Virus and his cohorts were currently serving twenty-five to life in the state penitentiary and the Torrance group had gone to ground. No one had been able to get Percy

Aljets on anything legally, but according to Doc, he was laying low and on his best behavior, especially since he wasn't able to completely get Brad off the hook in the prostitution ring.

Life could have only been described as blissful at the moment, and since we made the drive up to Atlanta every two or three months, Dash was much more settled on where his place was in the world.

I smacked his hands away. "Don't get me riled up right before I have to go and teach third graders…I need to be focused."

"I'll make up for it tonight," he promised. "Get you focused back on what's important."

"Can't wait," I said distractedly while I threw random things I thought I might need into my bag. I smoothed my hands down my brand-new jeans and bit my lip. "Do I look okay?"

"You look hot."

I sighed. "But do I look…teacherly?"

"Honestly? You don't look like any of my teachers in third grade. If I'd had you, I'd have been walking around with major wood all day long."

"Gross, Dash."

"Hey. You love my wood."

"Stop." I raised my hands in surrender and couldn't stop a giggle. "I have to get into teacher mode, not rip the clothes off my husband and take him on the kitchen floor mode."

"I could make that happen, baby. Just say the word."

I threw my hands in the air. "I give up."

Dash grinned. "You look beautiful and you'll be the best third grade teacher in that school…can't wait 'til our kids are goin' there."

"Me too."

"Come on, Mrs. Lloyd, it's time to face your students."

I grinned and grabbed my bag, taking a deep breath.

"I'm really proud of you, Willow," he said, kissing me. "You did everything you set out to do, and I'm in awe of you for it."

I stroked his cheek. "Thanks, honey. I'm pretty darn proud of you too, you know."

He smiled. "Yeah, you're good about telling me."

"I will never take you for granted."

"Ditto."

I kissed him again. "Okay, we need to go or I'll insist on you taking me back to bed."

"Got the keys, baby. I'm ready."

As I led him out of the house and he locked up, we climbed into the car and my man drove me to work. If you'd told me after everything that had happened three years ago, that I'd be married to my dream man, sporting a matching tattoo to cover our matching gunshot wounds (little band-aids with each other's names inscribed), and living the life of a biker's woman, I'd have laughed in your face.

But it was true and it was perfect.

ABOUT PIPER

Piper Davenport writes from a place of passion and intrigue, combining elements of romance and suspense with strong modern-day heroes and heroines.

She currently resides in pseudonymia under the dutiful watch of the Writers Protection Agency.

Like Piper's FB page and get to know her!
(www.facebook.com/piperdavenport)

Twitter: @piper_davenport

Made in the USA
Middletown, DE
20 March 2024

51386534R00119